QUEEN OF SNOW

FAIRYTALES REIMAGINED BOOK 1

LAURA BURTON
JESSIE CAL

BURTON & BURCHELL LTD

COPYRIGHT

DEDICATION

This series is written especially for fans of Once Upon a Time, who need more thrilling adventures, true love's kisses and good triumphing over evil. Shout out to our followers on the Fairytales Reimagined Facebook page. Without your enthusiasm and support, we wouldn't be able to do what we do! Thank you.

Laura & Jessie XoXo

BLURB

After falling through a magical mirror, Jack stumbles into the Chanted Forest, where fairy-tale characters are real...

He's rescued by Aria, a princess on the run from the evil queen, and together they embark on a quest to gather shards of a mirror so they can use the portal to get away from the Chanted Forest forever.

They will need the help of friends such as Belle, Robin, and Ryding Hood if they have any hope of surviving the deadliest of foes.

But when dark secrets unravel, Jack and Aria must make a difficult choice: Face an evil queen and save the kingdom? Or save themselves and leave the fairy tale characters without their happily ever after?

JACK

*J*ack bowed his head and clasped his hands together as he tried to block out the mass of mourners surrounding him. He was not bothered by the winter chill in the air. Nor did he notice the solemn drone from the pastor who stood at the head of the open grave.

Numb. He was numb. Void of emotion and entirely accepting that now his grandfather was gone, he was all alone.

Jack Smith was an only child, orphaned before he could walk and raised by his grandfather, Arthur Smith, who was a scholar and philosopher. Arthur was renowned by the whole of England for having published countless books and left behind a stately home which had an extensive library.

Jack had been homeschooled and hidden in the shadow of his grandfather's achievements all of his life. For seventeen years he had lived on the earth and never achieved anything remarkable on his own. And until now, he was just fine with that.

Jack knew it was time to move forward and figure out who he was, and what type of man he wanted to become.

But none of that mattered right now. In that moment, all Jack thought about was getting through the next couple of hours.

He threw a red rose into the grave; it hit the walnut coffin with a thud, and his eyes prickled.

"Goodbye, Grandfather," he whispered.

The people jostled beside him and took their turn to pay their respects. Jack shuffled back a little, stumbling on the uneven grass, and his ice-blue eyes shot up.

Standing in the distance, looking at another grave, stood a young woman no older than Jack. Her narrow shoulders trembled, and she wore a long ivory gown. Embroidered lace covered her arms, and she had a snowy white veil covering her blonde hair.

She stuck out in a sea of black. Like a single white rose among a bed of thorns.

Jack's gaze lingered on the young woman, wondering why she was alone and whom she was mourning. Then she looked up, and a spark of recognition fired in his brain as their eyes met.

Even though they were standing at least twenty feet apart, it was as if an invisible cord connected them, and a jolt of electricity shot through Jack.

He gasped and stepped away, breaking eye contact. As if it had severed the cord, his body returned to a numb state.

He recovered himself and scanned the cemetery to look at the young woman again. But she was gone.

"Look. It's snowing. Bob, how long have we lived here?" An old lady standing far off pointed to the thick, gray clouds. A sea of heads looked up.

"Good grief. You're right," an old man replied. "It hasn't snowed in Tynhem for over sixty years."

Tynhem was a little town just outside of Oxford, and in all of Jack's life, he had never seen it snow.

A dusting of white fell like ash from the sky and settled on the ground. Jack watched the flecks of snow fall into the open grave and allowed a slight smile to break his grimace. He knew his grandfather would have something philosophical to say about the moment. But Jack appreciated that, for once, the weather reflected his mood.

He whipped his head back and forth, searching the faces for the young woman he had seen just moments earlier. But she had vanished.

Slowly, the mourners walked back to the waiting cars, and Jack followed. Many of these people had known Jack's grandfather since before Jack was born, and yet no one so much as looked in his direction as they made their way to the manor for the wake.

Jack was grateful that Mr. Thomas had everything in hand. He took care of all the funeral arrangements, organized the caterers, and even booked a string quartet. It was above and beyond what any family lawyer should do. But he did it anyway. All Jack had to do was put on his suit and turn up.

The tires crunched over the gravel driveway as the stretch limousine pulled up outside the manor. A door opened and Jack stepped out gloomily. As he walked to the entrance, he stuffed his hands in his pockets and kept his head bowed low. Whispers flew around the courtyard and followed him into the home, but no one addressed him. He could have been invisible for all he knew.

A large stream of nosey people swarmed in and looked around the manor like they were visiting a museum. Arthur Smith was the grandson of a duke. The manor was the finest example of eighteenth-century architecture in Tynhem, and this was the first opportunity for members of the public to look inside.

According to the will, Arthur bestowed everything to Jack. But Jack did not like the idea of living in a twelve-bedroom manor and maintaining four acres of gardens alone. He instructed Mr. Thomas to sell it as soon as the funeral was over and let him know as soon as the funds were available.

What Jack would do next, or where he would go, remained a mystery. But he didn't care. This was no longer his home, and an unknown future called out to him.

After several awkward minutes of standing in the entrance hall, picking at the seam of his jacket, he headed upstairs to the bathroom, certain he would not be missed. He glanced at the paintings of his ancestors as he ascended the steps and allowed his hand to drag along the oak rail, rubbed smooth over years of use.

The floors creaked as he crossed the hall, and a sudden flash of light stopped him in his tracks. It came from his grandfather's office—a room Jack had been forbidden to ever step inside.

But unlike most days, the door was cracked open, and a light flashed again. Jack's curiosity piqued. *Just what was so special about Grandfather's office that I could never go inside?* he wondered. With a light shrug, he walked to the door and pushed it open.

No one was there to stop him this time.

The hinges squeaked as the door swung open and a flash of brilliant white light momentarily blinded him. Shielding his eyes, he cautiously stepped forward and blinked several times to take in the room. A wide mahogany desk stood proudly in the center with an open leather-bound book laying on top. Jack leaned in to find a quote encircled.

The best portion of a good man's life: his little name-less unremembered acts of kindness and love.

-William Wordsworth

Jack traced the words with his finger and let out a heavy sigh, but his breath caught in his throat. He tugged at his collar with a grimace and glanced at the small dusty window. He supposed it had never been opened.

The room was hot and stuffy, and Jack shrugged out of his jacket as he looked around. Many dusty shelves lined the walls, all sporting various antiques and artifacts. His grandfather's coat hung on a coat stand by the door, and a cane leaned against the desk. In the corner of the room stood an ornate free-standing oval mirror. The brass frame had etchings of words written in a language he did not recognize. Which was a surprise to him, as his grandfather had him study twelve languages, including Greek and Latin.

He caught his reflection. His muddy brown hair sat wavy around his ears, and despite his moody disposition, his eyes twinkled. He had always been scrawny and small, but the young man looking back at him in the mirror was taller, with a healthy glow. He stood up straight and squared his shoulders, clenching his biceps and setting his jaw. Then a pair of sky-blue eyes blinked at him from behind his shoulder. As quick as a flash, he turned to see who was standing behind him. He recognized those eyes. But no one was there.

Jack looked back at the mirror and took a step closer, his heart thumping and ears ringing.

Next to his head, he saw a spray of blonde hair obscuring a woman's eyes. He took another step and squinted. A delicate hand rose and brushed the strands of hair away from a porcelain face. His eyes lingered on a pretty pair of rosebud lips, and two glittering eyes met his gaze.

They held eye contact for a moment, then a blast of frosty air shot past Jack from the corner of the room. Startled, he stumbled forward, grasping the frame to find his balance.

He didn't dare to break eye contact with the woman in the reflection for fear that she might disappear again if he did.

Then a stronger blast hit him from behind. It was as if an unseen energy willed him to fall. Jack clutched the frame as his body went hurtling forward.

He braced for impact with the glass, but to his utter surprise, he fell through as if it was not a mirror at all, but an archway.

Shards of glass surrounded him and hung in the air, sparkling like glitter. Jack marveled at the sight, then another gust of air scattered them as far as the eye could see.

He stood on the top of a snowy hilltop, and brilliant white light flooded the sky. To the right, a magnificent white castle sparkled in the distance and a little village of wooden houses with smoking chimneys sat nestled in a valley.

Jack whipped around on the spot. The brass frame of the mirror lay in pieces at his feet, and his grandfather's office was nowhere to be seen.

"What the—?" he said in a breathy voice. Then he realized he was not alone. His brows shot up and his chest squeezed as he watched a young woman walking toward him. Her face looked the same as the woman he had seen in the mirror, but now her hair was brown.

Despite the winter frost, and the thin material of her cloak, she did not shiver. Nor were her cheeks rosy from the cold. She held out a gloved hand and smiled at Jack like she was an old friend. As if this was not the first time she had witnessed someone stumble through a mirror.

"Quickly," she said in a hushed voice, her smile fading as she grabbed his hand. Jack stumbled forward, his legs like jelly as he struggled to keep up. The young woman broke into a run, her feet flying across the snow with ease, cloak billowing out behind her. Jack's chest burned and the snow crunched under his feet.

"Wait. I can't—" he gasped and came to a halt. The young woman's eyes flashed as she stopped and looked at him with alarm.

"We can't stay here, Jack. We have to go."

Surprised at the sound of his name, Jack began moving again, and the two of them hurried down the hilltop towards the castle. All the while, the mystery woman kept her face forward, never so much as glancing back.

The ground leveled as they entered a woodland. Jack's lungs burned, and his legs refused to walk any further. He doubled over, gasping for air.

"We can't stop," the young woman urged. Jack looked up and frowned. How was she not out of breath? They had been running at full pelt for several minutes and his heart was about to burst out of his ribcage. Yet she hadn't broken a sweat.

"Who are you? How do you know my name?" he asked through gulping breaths. "And where am I?"

The young woman took a step closer, her warm breath tickling his forehead as she bent down to him. "You have a lot of questions. But for

JACK   11

now I only have one answer." Her voice was soft and musical and her words seemed to soothe his troubled soul. But then her eyes darkened.

"Trust no one." She threw her arm back in a swift motion, and struck him on the back of the head. Then everything went black.

ARIA

*T*he clouded winter sky cast a gloomy gray inside the tavern. Aria pulled her hood farther over her face as she sat at a corner table with an unlit candle. She watched the door, willing the pirate to arrive. The sooner she got this deal over with, the sooner she could get away. Guilt tugged at her heart no matter how much she avoided looking at the young man passed out next to her. Jack was his name, but it didn't matter. Soon enough he would be someone else's problem, and she would be closer to getting the only thing that mattered to her.

A group of dwarfs walked into the tavern with their faces downcast. They threw their axes on the floor with loud clunks before plopping down at the bar and ordering the strongest drink on the wall. A melodic sound seeped in through the open door, and Aria cringed. She hated mermaids, but the Chanted Forest was known for their enchanting songs sometimes carried by the wind over the whole kingdom.

"Brave choice," the man behind the bar said as he poured over a line of shot glasses. "What's the occasion?"

"Despair," a grumpy dwarf replied, snatching a glass and downing the drink. "Another!" As the man began to pour, the grumpy dwarf grabbed the bottle and slammed it on the counter. "Leave it."

"What has the queen done this time?" the man asked, finally realizing the source of their distress. She was, in fact, the source of everyone's anguish in the Chanted Forest.

"She set our village ablaze," another dwarf replied. "We came home to nothing but ashes."

"How many more villages will have to burn before this nightmare comes to an end?" A sleepy dwarf laid his head on the bar and stared at the liquid in his glass as if it were only a matter of time before the liquid also turned to ash.

"When she finally gets what she wants," the

grumpy dwarf replied with an angry growl. "The princess."

Aria lowered her head, using the hood to obscure her face. Not that they would have recognized her. Not only had she changed the color of her hair using the chemical of a plant, but the princesses were only displayed to the people on the day of their birth, then again on their eighteenth birthday. Had Aria still been at the palace, this year would've been her coronation ball.

She shook those thoughts out of her mind. That wasn't her life anymore, and there was no need to dwell on what could've been. It only made her heart ache, and she worked too hard in the past year to learn to control her emotions so as to keep her true identity hidden.

"What if we get her?" A dopey dwarf sat on top of the bar and faced his friends. "If it'll keep The Queen from burning more villages, then why not?"

"Because we don't know what the princess looks like," a dwarf with small round glasses replied, pushing aside his empty glass. "She could be dead for all we know. It's not likely a princess would survive alone out there."

"She better be dead," the grumpy dwarf said

with his jaw clenched. "Otherwise, she's nothing but a coward who allows everyone else to suffer at her expense."

Aria felt a stab in her chest. If they only knew what The Queen really wanted from her, they would understand that she wasn't hiding out of cowardice. She was protecting them like her father had taught her to do. And his courageous example was forever carved in her heart.

"Impressive," a deep voice approached her table, and she instinctively touched the knife she kept hidden under her cloak. "I was expecting less from you. After all, he isn't just a diamond necklace."

"You often underestimate me, Ryke," she said as he took a seat across from her. His piercing blue eyes suddenly locked on her while his black hair curved just above his brows. But his good looks didn't have any effect on her. "So, did you bring it?"

"You're quite feisty for a lass." He flashed her a charming smile that certainly could melt many hearts, but not hers. Hers was as cold as ice, and she liked it that way. Ryke then shifted his attention to Jack, who was still passed out on the table. "What did you do to the poor kid?"

"He's alive. Now, where's my payment?" Aria asked, firming her grip around the knife, just in case. "And I will take nothing less than what we agreed on."

"There's no need to be hostile, luv." Ryke gave an amused look as he lifted his arm to order a drink. "I'm a man of my word. I just need to make sure it's the correct merchandise."

He signaled with his arm again, and a young redhead boy with pointy ears came to sit next to Jack, his eyes glued to him as if he were a treasure chest full of jewels. Aria hated how they treated the young man like a pile of gold rather than a human being, but she forced herself to ignore it. After all, she hadn't treated him any differently.

"I didn't know pirates had dealings with elves." She noted the pointy ears.

Ryke took a gulp of his drink. "This pirate has dealings with the highest bidder."

She couldn't care less about his deals. "So…" Aria leaned her elbows on the table. "Do we have a deal or not?"

Ryke glanced at the elf as he examined Jack's face for a long moment. The elf looked up with a beaming smile, but Ryke still hesitated.

"It's okay," the elf assured him. "You can give it to her. It's really him."

Ryke then murmured in a different language. The elf responded, keeping his voice low as if that would make any difference. Aria didn't speak the language, but she did recognize the sound. And since Ryke was a pirate, it made sense they would be speaking the language of the sea. And since elves speak all languages, that wasn't surprising either.

Aria focused on what the elf was saying, and all she could make out was something about a *"espelho completo."*

She had no idea what it meant, but Ryke's eyes widened in surprise. Aria wondered what in the world had the elf said to eliminate Ryke's reservations. Without any further reluctance, he pulled out a crimson cloth from his jacket—it was the size of his large hand—and placed it on the table. "All right, lass. You've got yourself a deal."

Aria narrowed her eyes. Something didn't feel right.

"May I?" She pointed to the crimson cloth, and he pushed it toward her. She unwrapped the cloth until she spotted a shard of the mirror. But not just any mirror. She angled it where she could see her own reflection. The girl sitting in the tavern had brown hair, but the reflection staring back at her had glistening blonde hair, and that was how she knew the shard belonged to the Mirror of Reason.

She looked up to meet Ryke's dark blue eyes.

"Isn't that what you wanted, luv?" he asked, and she nodded. "Then we are done here." He turned around to order another drink while the redhead went through Jack's pockets.

Aria felt a sudden urge to stop him, but she clenched her fists and sucked in a deep breath. *You got what you wanted. Get up and walk away.* She wrapped the shard back in the crimson cloth then placed it carefully inside her bag. When she stood, she couldn't help stealing one last glance at Jack's face. He looked just as young as she did. Though his eyes were closed, she remembered its royal blue color so vividly. And as glad as she was to have gotten her hands on yet another shard of the Mirror of Reason, she couldn't stop the nagging feeling that there was more to this young man than she thought. Especially in the way he gazed at her when he first saw her. It was as if he knew her. But how? He wasn't even from this realm.

"Is there anything else we can do for you,

luv?" Ryke asked, looking up from his drink. When Aria didn't respond, he grabbed her wrist and pulled her down to him. "Then I suggest you go before you end up locked in the cage with him."

Aria yanked her arm free, and Ryke laughed. As much as she hated backing down from a challenge, she needed to get out of there. She'd drawn too much attention already.

By the time she left the tavern, the sky had grown dark and the smell of liquor filled the air. On her way down a dark alley, she spotted a group of drunk sailors speaking the same language she'd heard Ryke and the elf talking earlier.

"Hey!" she called out, and they all turned to look at her. "The language you're speaking… is it the language of the sea?"

One of the sailors stepped forward with a drunken grin. "I'll tell you only if you ask nicely."

Aria pushed the sailor against the wall then dug the tip of her knife into his throat. "How's this for nice?"

His eyes widened like two fried eggs, and when he gulped, she traced the tip of her blade over his Adam's apple. "Now… what does *espelho completo* mean?"

He gulped against her blade. "Complete mirror."

Aria gasped as she pulled back, and the group of drunken men scattered, leaving her alone in the alley. She put her knife away, then leaned against the wall. Now it made sense why they gave her the shard. Whoever Jack was, he had access to the completed mirror. Or at least, that was what it sounded like.

Whatever the case, she needed to get Jack back. And in order to do so, she was going to need her bow and arrow… and her horse.

JACK

*J*ack stirred, blinking against the throbbing pain behind his eyes and rubbed the back of his head, remembering the strangest dream.

A beautiful woman knocked him over the head and carried him to a bar. Some sort of exchange was made and he was dragged into a carriage. What followed was a wildly uncomfortable ride where his captors rambled on in Portuguese about a mirror. The rest of the details were hazy, but he was pretty sure someone forced a cloth over his mouth as he wrestled to break free, and then everything grew dark again.

He sat up and frowned at the uncomfortable bench he had been sleeping on. It was certainly a far cry from the orthopedic mattress he had in his own room.

The logical side of his brain concocted a story that he had consumed too much alcohol at the wake—the devastation of loss all-consuming—and collapsed in one of the dining rooms at the manor.

Jack was not one to drink. But it would definitely explain the crazy dreams and his headache.

He shuffled off the bench, and his shoes landed on a hardwood floor. He wrinkled his nose at the moldy aroma of his surroundings and squinted into the darkness. He cleared his throat and the sound echoed. His heart sank.

Perhaps it was *not* a dream after all.

As his eyes adjusted to the darkness, a faint outline of his surroundings came into view. He was still in the carriage. Flecks of snow flurried through a pair of iron bars and landed at his feet. Jack coughed against the thickness in the air and tried to make sense of his predicament.

If he was truly awake, then, Jack *fell* through the mirror in his grandfather's office and landed… somewhere very cold. But *where*, exactly?

He staggered over to the bars and grasped

the cold iron with shaking hands. The roughness of the surface grazed his palms, but Jack welcomed the sensation. It reminded him that he was alive. At least for now. He peered through the bars to catch a glimpse of a dark forest.

Did his grandfather know about the magical mirror? Had he ever used it as a portal to another world? He cast his mind back and remembered it was not unusual for his grandfather to barricade himself in his study for days—weeks even.

Why didn't he tell Jack about it? And now that the mirror was broken—he did see billions of glass fragments scatter, after all—how would he return home?

Then he remembered the beautiful woman's face. Her porcelain skin, almond-shaped eyes, and flowing hair. But in a flash, her ice-blue eyes darkened and her expression soured.

"Trust no one."

It had been almost a growl, a stark contrast to her warm and musical voice. It had caught Jack by surprise. Before he had known what was happening, he was being sold. All for what? He hadn't seen. He had thought it best to keep his eyes shut and pretend to be unconscious. Who was this woman and what did she want so badly that had driven her to kidnap him?

He inwardly reprimanded himself for falling so easily for the girl's charm. Had he not known better than to blindly follow a woman to his doom after venturing into the beyond? He slammed a fist against the bars and then winced as the deafening twang rang in his ears at full volume.

The squeal of a rusty hinge drew his attention, and the steady thud of boots hitting the cobbled path had him on edge.

"Where does the master want us to take him?"

"For now, to the ship."

He stepped back as the stench of stale sweat and liquor wafted his way. What did these men want with him? And who was their *master*?

Jack swallowed as he listened to the jingle of keys, then a click. The carriage door flung open, revealing a man wearing black leather boots, a pair of breeches and a gray waistcoat over a cotton shirt. He had a short beard and wore a hat to complete the look. Though Jack had never seen the man in his life, he knew what he was. A pirate.

"Tie him up," the pirate said gruffly. A redhead appeared and shuffled forward, grabbing Jack's arms. Too bewildered and frozen to move,

Jack didn't fight back. "Keep your mouth shut." The pirate leaned into the carriage and growled into his ear. Were these people here to save him? His situation was so far beyond logic and reason, he figured at this point, anything was possible. He gave a curt nod and the pirate sneered as the redhead tied his hands.

A scratchy sack was forced over his head, and then the carriage door slammed. Moments later, the carriage moved forward, and all Jack could hear was the steady clip-clop of the horses' hooves.

The chill of the air had a bite to it. Yet a distant howl grew into a ferocious roar as an icy cold gust of wind hit the carriage. Despite the jostling and frosty weather, Jack was calm. He had always been fond of the cold.

He heard the cry from a far-off bird and set his jaw. If only he could have transformed into a bird and flown away to freedom.

The carriage came to an abrupt stop and the whinny of the horses had Jack's heart racing. He caught the sound of a whistle in the air, followed by a grunt and a heavy thud against the door, causing the carriage to jolt sideways.

"What in the blazes...?" a man outside

muttered. Then the man cried out and the carriage lurched to the side as something heavy collided with it.

Jack's senses were on high alert. His ears picked up the crunching gravel as quickening steps circled the carriage. Then a scuffle of movement at his side. With trembling hands, he dragged the sack from his face and took a breath. He heard a symphony of sounds: the clash of steel blades, the thump of flesh making contact with the path, and a distant whistle.

He staggered to the iron bars as an arrow landed with a thud just inches away from his nose. He glimpsed a hooded figure deep in battle with the dark-haired pirate. They moved with such grace and agility, it was almost like a dance. But it ended when the hooded figure pinned the pirate to the tree and hit him on the head with a piece of wood from the broken carriage.

A strange and eerie silence followed as the figure turned around.

Jack stumbled out of the carriage with his hands still tied and awkwardly staggered to find his balance.

"Stop moving."

Jack craned his neck at the familiar voice. The

cold steel of a blade slid between his hands, and in a swift action, his bonds fell to the ground. Jack jumped to his feet and stumbled away from the hooded figure.

"It's you!"

The figure threw their hood back to reveal the brunette from the hilltop. Her eyes shifted left and right, then narrowed at him.

"We have to move," she said, putting away her knife then shrugging a bow onto her shoulder as she looked at the immobile bodies on the ground. "It's not safe. There could be more of them." She grunted as she tugged at the arrow embedded in the flank of one of the bodies and wiped it on her cloak. Jack folded his arms.

"You sold me to them."

The young woman glared at him. "And now I'm saving you." She whistled, and a gray gelding galloped out from the tree line. "Besides, I have a horse. And you won't get far on foot."

Jack was just about to argue that he could take one of the horses from the carriage when he noticed they had bolted. He sighed heavily as he considered his options. It was bitterly cold, he had no idea where he was, nor where to go, and it seemed like an age since his last meal.

The woman was right. He wouldn't even last a day.

"Will you at least tell me who these people are? What do they want with me?" Jack asked as he rubbed his wrists and rolled his shoulders. The young woman mounted the horse and held out her hand for him.

"I'll tell you everything I know, but we have to go now." She gave him a look so pleading, he almost didn't recognize the fighter he'd just seen beating up his captors. Jack took her hand and climbed on. The horse neighed, and without another word the woman kicked and they charged into the forest.

*J*ack was inquisitive at the best of times, but now the inner workings of his mind were doing overtime. So many questions burned within that if he did not have answers soon, he might burst into flames.

Growing up in his grandfather's shadow, no one had had any time for Jack. He had lived a somewhat solitary life. When he was a small child, the only company he had day to day was a small fly that lived in his room. He escaped into new worlds, reading all of the books in the library—Jack's favorite place in the manor. He was particularly fond of the classic fairy tales. He knew even the most obscure ones by heart. As William Wordsworth had said:

Dreams, books, are each a world.

And Jack had many dreams and read many books. So, he argued that he had traveled farther than most. Yet if he took his recent experiences and applied them to the books he had read, his conclusion was that he had somehow stumbled into the stories. Had there not been dwarves at the pub? But the thought was implausible. Perhaps he was still buried deep in a drunken sleep. The latter made more sense.

The horse sped up and darted into the woodland. Jack sucked in air between his teeth as they raced through the overgrown trees, narrowly missing claw-like branches from all sides. The woods had a mystical and unearthly atmosphere under the moonlight.

Yet the woman remained quiet and confident, murmuring the horse instructions as if the horse was not an animal, but a comrade.

Jack held her narrow waist. "Are you talking to the horse?"

"It's a little trick my sister taught me."

Jack silently thanked his grandfather for insisting on years of horse riding lessons. Otherwise, this bumpy ride might have been much more of a challenge.

The horse galloped faster, and the wind howled in Jack's ears. His questioning brain froze as the sculpture-like trees blurred in his peripheral vision and the wind ruffled his hair. Every atom in Jack's body buzzed as if they had become the winter storm.

He did not know where they were headed, nor if they were going to ride all night. But Jack was determined to get answers. And somehow he knew that this mystery woman was the key to finding them.

After all, she was the reason he fell through the mirror.

ARIA

Other than the fire crackling in front of them, the night was fairly quiet. The light of the flames revealed the charred black trees. The once-bustling village of taverns and homes was now a desolate land dotted with piles of ashes.

Aria broke a loaf of bread in half and handed it to Jack. He grabbed it from her like a famished animal, and she suddenly felt bad for not waking him up at the tavern to eat something.

"I'm sorry there isn't much to eat," she said, pulling off her gloves and leaning closer to the fire. "I thought there would still be a village here."

Jack studied her as he leaned back against a thick log. "What happened?"

Aria looked around, taking in the scattered ashes, the distinct smell burning the back of her throat. But before her eyes could fill with tears, she turned her attention back to the flames.

"Seems that she burned it down."

"Wait. A whole village? Who would do such a thing?" Jack's eyes darted left and widened, as if only now taking in their charred surroundings.

"The Queen," Aria replied with a distaste in her mouth. "That's usually how she gets what she wants."

Jack was silent for a long moment as he stared into the burning fire. Aria studied the intense expression as the reflection of the flames danced across his thoughtful face.

"And what does she want?" he finally asked. Aria hesitated. She didn't like talking about it. But she could see Jack was a deep thinker. If she didn't respond—or avoided the subject entirely—he would most likely connect the dots.

"The princess," she said. "She ran away a year ago."

"Why?"

"All we know is there used to be two king-doms," she explained, leaning closer to the fire. "The Chanted Forest was under the rule of King

Dario and his wife for many decades. It was wonderful living here. Until the queen from the north came and wiped out his whole family." Aria willed herself not to cry. "The princess was the only one who escaped."

"That's terrible," Jack gasped. "Where do you think she is now?"

"Not here, that's for sure." She took another bite out of her bread. "If she was, I'm pretty sure The Queen's men would've found her by now. She's got eyes everywhere."

"Maybe those men who took me work for her," Jack said, suddenly alarmed. But Aria let out an unconcerned chuckle.

"Trust me, Ryke does not work for The Queen."

"What makes you so sure?" he asked.

"Ryke is too arrogant and quite mouthy," she said, still chuckling. "The Queen would have him killed in no time."

"Well then, who do they work for?"

"I don't know." And that was the truth. The extent of Aria's business with Ryke was meeting at the tavern and selling stolen goods. That was it. Aria had never even been to his ship.

"Then tell me something you *do* know," Jack

pressed. "Why did you save me back there? What do *you* want from me?"

Aria hesitated, but only for a moment. "The Mirror of Reason."

Jack gave her a puzzled look. "Mirror of what?"

She gave him an annoyed look. She was not in the mood to play games. "The mirror that you used to come to our land."

Jack sat up, suddenly intrigued. "Wait... you know I'm not from here?"

"Of course." Aria pointed at his clothes. "We don't have anything like that here."

He looked at himself then up at Aria again.

"So that mirror was some sort of portal?"

Aria arched a brow as Jack looked at himself again. He touched his chest and arms as if he couldn't believe his flesh was real.

"How is that possible?"

"I was hoping you would tell me. I've never been through one before." When he looked up at her again, the reflection of the fire danced in his puzzled eyes.

"I was in my grandfather's study when I saw..." He paused, and Aria leaned closer, clinging to his every word. But then there was a change in his tone and Aria could tell he was hesitant.

"Saw what?" she pressed.

"The mirror," he said quickly. "I saw the mirror."

She had a nagging suspicion that wasn't his first thought but didn't press it. "And what did you do?"

"I just looked at it for a while, then I noticed…" He paused again with the same look in his eyes.

What was he hiding?

He shook his head. "It doesn't matter. I only remember a gust of wind and losing my balance."

"And then what happened?" Though she'd read much about the mirror in the last year, there was much still unknown. Sure, she was collecting shards to put one together, but she had never actually seen or used a completed one before.

"The mirror shattered, and I was at the hilltop standing in front of you." He held her gaze for a long moment. "How did you know where to find me? I mean, you were there the moment I fell through."

"Ryke…" she whispered to herself, then shook her head. "But it doesn't make any sense. If you fell through the portal by accident, how did he know you were coming? He told me exactly where you would be. Jack, he even told me your name."

The softness in his eyes stirred up a sense of familiarity. As if they had known each other all their lives. The sense of calm she got from his presence bothered her. She wasn't used to feeling comfortable with anyone.

"You still haven't told me *your* name," he said, catching Aria by surprise.

She broke her gaze abruptly and pulled back. "We should get some sleep," she said, slipping her hands back into her gloves then turning away from him. "It's going to be a long day tomorrow—"

"Aria." His voice was barely above a whisper, but it landed on her ears like a thunderstorm. She jumped to her feet and moved away from him.

"How did you do that?" she asked, but he seemed just as surprised as she was.

"I have no idea," he muttered. "I just… knew."

She pulled her knife from her sheath, and Jack jumped to his feet. "You just *knew*?"

"Hold on a minute..." He raised his hands defensively, a look of genuine concern on his face.

"I have no idea what is going on here, but I'm not a threat. If anything, I have more questions than answers." He let out an exhausted sigh then dropped his hands. "I just need to find a way to go back, and as crazy as this may sound... I have a feeling you're the only one who can help me."

"Why is that?"

When he opened his mouth but didn't respond, she could tell there was more he wasn't letting on. But it wouldn't do any good to beat it out of him. Reasoning seemed like a better tactic to get through a guy like Jack.

"I need to know what happened to that mirror," he finally said. "And you seem to know a lot about it. So, what do you say? Will you help me?"

The honesty in his voice pulled at her heart-strings. She knew the ache of missing home, and the hollow look in his eyes took her back to a year ago when she had no choice but to leave her family behind. Especially her sister.

"Okay." She lowered her weapon. "I'll help you, but I'm gonna need something in return."

"You name it."

"I also want to use the mirror to leave this realm."

"Deal." He stretched out his hand, and she took it. "You have my word. Scout's honor."

"What's that?"

Jack smiled. "I think the more pressing question is… how do we find out what happened to my grandfather's mirror?"

"Right." She released his hand and sheathed her knife. "I have a friend who has read pretty much every book ever written. If there's anyone who would know how to get you back home, it would be her. Now…" Aria grabbed a bag from off the horse and pushed it into Jack's chest. "Get some sleep. We'll leave at sunrise."

⁂

They clung to Aria's gray horse as they galloped toward the manor, only slowing to a canter when they crossed the stone bridge.

"Is that where we're going?" Jack asked, mesmerized by the beauty of the dark gray structure.

It made her smile since that manor was not even half the size of what her palace used to be.

But she shook the thought from her mind. That life wasn't hers anymore.

"We're going to see a good friend," Aria said, guiding the horse into the woods and around the side of the manor. "Her name is Belle. And if she's here, she'll be in the library."

"Belle?" Jack sounded surprised. "She lives here?"

"No, she just takes care of the place while the owner is away."

"But The Beast had a castle," he mumbled to himself.

"What beast?" Aria asked with an arched brow. "And how in the world would you know anything about Belle?"

"I don't," he said quickly. "I was just thinking of a book I read growing up. Fascinating story."

"Sure sounds like it." She stopped the horse under a tree, but before she could dismount, Jack jumped down then turned to face her. He stretched out his arms like a gentleman to catch her, and the gesture caught her off guard.

"Since we're working together, it would be good to start trusting each other," Jack said, keeping his arms outstretched. "Go on."

"Fine." She jumped into his arms, and he

caught her effortlessly. But when his deep blue eyes met hers, something flipped in the pit of her stomach. "All right." She pushed him away then smoothed down her cloak. "Happy now?"

Jack smiled, but she couldn't understand what was so amusing to him. Could he sense how vulnerable he made her feel? She couldn't let her guard down. She wouldn't. She turned away from him and reached for her bow and arrows. After strapping the quiver securely around her chest, he stepped in front of her.

"Shouldn't I carry a weapon?" he asked.

"Why?" The corner of her lips lifted in light mockery. "Are you afraid there's a beast in there?" she teased, checking to make sure her knife was still in her sheath. "Seems these tales you've read in your kingdom have scarred you quite deeply. Worry not. Things are a lot simpler here."

Jack pulled back, chuckling. "If you only knew the irony of your words, it would be quite humorous."

"Good thing I'm not in the mood to laugh. Now, let's go."

After sneaking through the bushes, Aria led the way toward a small wooden door. She wasn't surprised to find it open. She peeked inside and spotted a petite woman with light brown hair tied into a braid, sitting with her back to them at a large table in the center of the room. Every inch of the walls around her was covered with books.

"Gotcha, Belle," Aria said loud enough for the maiden to hear as she stepped inside.

"Aria!" Belle flashed a beaming smile as she rushed around the table to wrap Aria in a tight hug. "It's so good to see you! And who's this?" Her hazel eyes rested curiously on Jack, who was gazing up at the bookshelves.

Aria pulled back and stepped aside to introduce Jack, but he was too distracted to notice. His whole face beamed like a child with candies.

"Jack?"

"Yes?" He came over to them, his face radiating with joy. "I was miles away for a moment there." He offered his hand, and Belle took it. "Pleasure to meet you, Belle. I'm Jack." He craned his neck up and pointed to the vast rows of leather-bound books. "What a magnificent collection. It's quite impressive."

"You like to read?" Belle asked, surprised. "It's not often I see young men such as yourself interested in books." Her eyes flitted down his body and settled on Jack's face again with her brows

raised. Which reminded Aria to find Jack a
change of attire.

"Well, I'm not from around here," Jack
replied. "In fact, that's why we came to see you.
Aria tells me you may know a way to help me
home."

"And where is home?" Belle asked, turning to
Aria. "And how exactly can I be of assistance?"

"He came through a mirror," Aria said with a
pointed look, and Belle's eyes widened.

"You completed the mirror?"

"No… he came through his *own* mirror. From
another realm."

"Another mirror…" Belle whispered to herself
as she began to pace the room. Then she stopped
and looked at Jack, her face lit up with excite-
ment. "So it's true. There are other mirrors… in
different realms."

"Yes," Aria confirmed. "I saw him come
through with my own eyes."

"What happened to the mirror? Did it come
with you?" Belle asked as she hurried to one of
the bookshelves.

"It shattered as soon as I landed here," Jack
said, following after her with Aria by his side.

"What happened to the shards?" Belle asked,

not bothering to turn around as she continued scanning the spine of each book.

"There were thousands of tiny shards everywhere," Jack said. "Then they scattered and disappeared."

"That's good," Belle said. "Here it is!" She pulled a book from the shelf and brought it to the table. Aria and Jack came to look over her shoulder and watched as she flipped through the pages quickly, knowing exactly what she was looking for. "Here..."

Jack and Aria leaned closer. "What language is that?" Aria asked.

"The language of the sea." Belle pointed to the top of the page. "And here is the only reference of the mirror in this book, but it explains exactly what happened. It says—"

"After we had traveled through the mirror, it seemed the glass had become like sparkling grains of sand, before the wind took them and they vanished. But the mirror had not broken, it was a mere side effect. Some would call a hallucination…"

By the time Jack finished translating, Belle and Aria were staring at him in shock.

"How do you speak the language of the sea?" Aria asked.

"It's called Portuguese where I'm from," he explained. "My grandfather made me study languages, but that's not important. This is…" He picked up the book, and after rereading the paragraph, he turned to Belle. "So, this means that the mirror is still intact in my land."

Belle nodded. "But there's no way of getting to it from here," she added. "The only way to go back is to use another mirror."

"Where would we find another mirror?" Jack asked. "I thought you said the one here is shattered?"

Belle's eyes flickered to Aria for a tenth of a second. But it was enough for Jack to notice. "You can't be serious." He turned to Aria as if she'd slapped him. "You have a mirror?"

"Not a whole one," Aria confessed. "I have been collecting shards and trying to piece one together, though." She dug into her satchel and pulled out the crimson cloth. "This is what I sold you for." She handed it to him and watched as he unwrapped it on the table. "They gave it away because they probably thought they could get the full mirror from you. As did I."

"How far are you from completing it?" he

asked, and she leaned back on the table next to him.

"I think it only needs two more shards, but it's hard to be sure," she said, looking at Belle, who was again scanning through the bookshelf. "Would you know where to find them?"

"Last I heard, the ogres had one. You know how they love to collect shiny objects," Belle said, pulling another book from the shelf and bringing it to the table. "But there is one more thing about the mirror you should know." She opened the book to the middle and scanned it line by line until she found what she was looking for.

"Is it in common language?" Aria asked, and Belle smiled.

"Yes." She pointed to the sentence and waited for Aria to read it aloud.

"*One broken mirror. Seven years of bad luck.*" Aria stared at the page as if waiting for an explanation, but there was nothing. She looked up from the book with an annoyed look. "Great. It's a flipping riddle."

She threw the book on the table, and Jack snatched it up like a newborn baby. He gave her an affronted look at her carelessness, then he examined it with his brows furrowed. "Of course..." he murmured, turning to Belle. "If the mirror is cracked, it can only be used once every seven years."

"But why the bad luck?" Aria asked.

"Imagine being stuck in another realm for seven years. Being cut off from everyone you know sounds like bad luck to me," he explained, but Aria didn't see the bad luck in that. Leaving the Chanted Forest and getting away from everyone she knew was exactly what she wanted. But apparently not Jack. Closing the book, he placed it back on the table then stared at the closed cover intently as if willing it to solve all of his problems.

Before she realized what she was doing, her hand was already on his shoulder. "Are you all right?" she asked.

"My grandfather had a portal to another world, and he never told me." Though his voice was barely above a whisper, the pain in his tone was clear. "All the books he had me read about explorers. All the ancient myths and legends he made me study. The languages he made me learn. The horseback riding lessons. Everything. It was as if he was preparing me for this place somehow, but yet... He never told me about it." When he looked at her again, the mixture of hurt and confusion in his eyes was so intense that Aria ached inside. "Why didn't he tell me? Did he not *trust* me?"

She cupped his face in her hands, and when she held his gaze, her heart squeezed for him. "My mother always told me that *we are the authors of our own fate.* So, you can sit here and try to understand why your grandfather kept things from you. Or you can write your own fate. Maybe… there's something here for you, after all."

"Maybe there is…" he whispered. "After all, with Grandfather gone, there's not much for me in England." When his eyes dropped to her lips, she felt an explosion of butterflies in her stomach.

Belle dropped a stack of books on the floor, and both Jack and Aria swung around to see what was wrong. She gaped at Jack like a fish out of water.

"Did you say England?" she asked, her fingers resting on her collarbone.

"Yes," he said, giving Belle a quizzical look. "Have you heard of it?"

"Once," she said, picking the books from the floor. "Years ago, I met a man who said he'd come from England. He gave me this." She put the books on the table and pulled out her necklace so Jack could see.

"What is it?" Aria asked.

"It's an English coin. An old one, too," Jack answered. "See the face? That's Queen Victoria."

Belle nodded. "Right. Well, the same thing that happened to you, happened to him. And he came to my village looking for mirror shards. At the time, I had one in my possession, and he made a deal with me."

"What kind of deal?" Jack asked.

"If I gave him the shard, he would tell me how I could find true love and happiness without any heartache." She chuckled wryly, as if she knew how absurd it sounded. "I have no idea where he got it, but he had a book with all of our fates in them."

"You read the book?" Jack asked.

"Only my story."

When she ran a finger over the inside of her arm, Jack stared at the large scar from the inside of her wrist to her elbow.

"May I?" he said, holding out his hand. Belle's hazel eyes shot down before she nodded. Jack gently took her arm and turned it to get a better look at it. "The Beast was never supposed to hurt you."

Belle nodded, still staring at the scar. "The Intruder changed my fate. And I wasn't the only one. Over the years, I heard rumors that he's rumpled a lot of lives. He's come to be known as The Intruder."

"What happened to him?" Jack asked.

"Nobody's seen him for years. But if I ever find him..." Belle's eyes turned dark for a moment. "Well, let's just say The Beast will be the least of his worries."

"Wait..." Aria shook her head as if she hadn't heard them correctly. "So, there really is a beast?"

"You both should go." Belle glanced at the wooden clock on the wall, then started closing the books on the table. "Tonight is a full moon and you should get as far away from these woods as possible."

When Belle turned around to put the books back on the shelf, Jack turned to Aria. "Full moon? She doesn't mean…?" he whispered.

Aria nodded.

"Wolves," she whispered back. "During my stay with Robin and his cousin, Ryding Hood, I've been on the receiving end of those attacks, and it's not pretty." She walked over to Belle and pulled her into a hug. "Thank you for all your help."

"Anytime."

"May I wash up for a second before we go?" Aria asked, taking the crimson cloth with the shard and placing it back inside her satchel.

"Sure. I'll prepare a basket of food for you both," Belle said. "It's a two-day journey to the ogres' swamp."

Aria left Jack talking with Belle about books and went to the washroom. She entered the small room made of rocks and pottery and turned to face the mirror. After pulling off her gloves, a wave of ice shot out of her hands, freezing the metal tub in the corner. She balled them into fists then took in a deep breath. How much longer was it going to take for her to fully control her powers?

Within a few seconds, she opened her frost-covered hand and placed them under the running water. The ice melted and she washed her face— sighing at the splash of cold water against her warm skin. She wet her hair then twisted it in a bun using a piece of broken arrow to keep up. As she faced the mirror, her eyes landed on the stone necklace around her neck, and memories of her mother came flooding back. Her heart squeezed so tightly, she grabbed onto the basin. It froze within seconds, and she pressed her eyes shut. Tears threatened to break through, but she clenched her jaw and willed herself to hold it together.

As she stared at her reflection in the mirror, it was hard to recognize the person looking back. So much had changed in a year. So much had been lost in so little time. She had everything, then in the blink of an eye, it was all gone.

That did make her decision to leave that much easier, even if she did end up stuck in a strange realm for seven years. Anywhere else would be better than staying in the Chanted Forest. If she were to get caught, it wasn't her own life she would be putting at risk. It was the entire kingdom.

She splashed more cold water on her face, but when she lifted her head, her eyes locked with one of The Queen's men standing behind her. Before she could react, he grabbed her by the neck and pressed her back against his black-armored chest.

"Hi there, Princess," he hissed into her ear. "Going somewhere?"

JACK

"Thanks for the change of clothes, Belle." Jack returned to the kitchen wearing thick cotton pants and a shirt. He shrugged on a sheepskin jacket and wriggled his toes in his new leather boots. He tossed his funeral clothes in the burning fire, happy to see them go up in smoke.

"So, what happened to The Beast?" he asked, still staring into the flames licking at the clothes.

Belle didn't answer and a shift in the air had Jack on edge. He looked up and spun around, catching sight of two men in black armor apprehending Belle.

"What the—?"

Before he could collect his thoughts, a metal

hand punched him in the side. He doubled over, dropping the book on the floor, then two more men grabbed his arms.

"Let's take a walk," one of them snarled in his ear.

The men frog-marched Belle and Jack out of the library and down the hall. Jack thought it best not to fight since they were outnumbered and he was unarmed. The only weapon he had was his mind, and it started to work overtime. Who were these men, and what did they want with them?

He glanced at the oil paintings on the stone walls, and suits of armor lining the hall. He wondered how quickly he could grab one of their swords and how many men he could fight at once. It would most certainly be different from his fencing lessons, but could he pull it off? He inwardly shook himself. No, he was no action hero. And he couldn't risk Belle getting hurt if he failed.

They entered a ballroom, not dissimilar to the one illustrated in the book he had read about Belle. It had a painted dome ceiling, and extravagant chandeliers, twinkling like stars in the night sky. Silver moonlight poured through stained glass windows from above.

They descended the large staircase, the sound of boots thudding against the cold floors echoed around the room as they reached the center.

"Get on your knees," one of the men barked.

Jack made eye contact with a terrified Belle and gave her a reassuring nod. They lowered themselves to the floor at the same time, and the men stood around them like guards. As if they were waiting for something.

A distant scream made Jack tense up. *Aria.* He balled his fists and set his jaw, thinking the poor girl must be frightened. He wondered how fast his captors could run in their heavy suits of armor. He was confident he would be faster. But if Jack bolted, what would happen to Belle?

There was a sudden chill in the air, like all of the fires in the castle had been extinguished and someone opened all of the windows at the same time. Belle shivered at his side, and the men dragged them behind the piano, ordering them to be silent. Screams came from down the hall, followed by a crash and the sound of metal clanging to the floor. Jack's chest throbbed as his heart beat against his ribs like a drum, wondering if perhaps the beast was coming?

A door upstairs burst open, and in an instant,

the wooden banister turned to ice. A group of the guards charged up the staircase, but slipped as the marble froze beneath their feet. A small hooded figure dashed across the upper hall and appeared on the top of the stairs, standing powerful. Then the hood fell back, and Jack gasped.

Aria.

She was nimble like a cat as she hurried down the icy steps, taking two and a time. She outstretched a hand and a blast of ice shot out like a fountain and crystalized on the marble floor. The fallen guards staggered to their feet, swords raised as they approached her, but Aria was too fast for them. She dodged their attacks, ducked under their arms, and then clamped a hand on them. Within a blink of an eye, two of the guards became statues of ice.

Jack grinned, but the grin collapsed into a frown at the sudden pressure on his neck. He swallowed against the cold metal.

"I wouldn't do that if I were you."

Aria turned away from the frozen guards and her face paled. She raised her hands as yet another guard approached from behind. Then he clamped a silver bracelet on her wrist.

"At least now we know she's the real princess,"

one of the guards said with a dark laugh. "Get her in the cage."

Aria wrestled against the guard as he bound her hands behind her back and shot Jack a pointed look. He stared at her, still reeling from the shock of her powers.

Did they just call her a princess?

Aria was the princess. The one The Queen was burning villages down to find. So, the guards must have been hired by The Queen.

"What shall we do with these two?"

The tallest guard removed his helmet, then stared back with soulless eyes before he said in a flat voice, "Kill them."

Jack's survival instincts kicked in. He grabbed the blade, ignoring the pain as it slit his skin open. He jerked forward with so much force, the guard fell flat on the floor with a tremendous crash.

The cold air picked up like a storm in the room, encircling them as they were still on their knees. Jack rose to his feet. A ferocious wind howled and the windows shattered, showering them all with tiny glass fragments. The guards looked at each other and staggered back, trying to stay upright against the unearthly force. Belle was released and Jack pulled her toward him.

"Come on!" he shouted, running toward Aria, who had already taken down the three guards around her. Belle shielded her eyes as they pushed against the wind as if trying to cross a frozen lake in a blizzard.

The three of them trudged forward while the guards fell back. The weight of their armor was too great.

Once outside, the winds died down.

"We have to keep moving," Jack said as he untied Aria. She pulled away and put on her gloves, looking at Jack with alarm.

"The horse. Come on. This way—" she said, but Belle grabbed her arm and gave her a hard look.

"You go on. I'll hold them off," she said.

"Are you sure—"

"Trust me." Belle smiled. "I just need to let someone out."

The two of them embraced, then Aria nodded as they broke apart. She looked at Jack. "We have to go. Now!" she said.

Jack thanked Belle, but Aria kept tugging on his hand as the guards shouted from the castle.

"Seize her!"

Jack and Aria ran at full pelt across the dark

castle grounds, never looking back. The winds picked up again, as if the elements were on their side, and the ferocious gales kept a distance between them and the guards.

When they found Aria's horse, he was munching on apples, unaware of any urgency. Jack helped Aria up, then climbed on behind her. Suddenly, the howling of a wolf echoed in the distance and they looked at each other in fear. When the guards screamed, Jack grabbed the reins from Aria and willed the horse to move, galloping back into the woods.

A long time had passed when they finally slowed and Jack's breathing returned to normal. They stopped by a river and Aria climbed down, hurling her knife on the ground with an angry grunt. She'd been trying to remove the bracelet from her arm all night, but with no luck.

"We'll rest here for an hour," she said, still avoiding Jack's eyes. "Pepper needs a break." She stooped down to the water with a sheepskin flask.

Jack jumped down and led the horse to the

river's edge. Then he sat on the bank and looked at his hands while Aria removed the saddle from the horse. Now that the adrenaline was gone, an uncomfortable burning sensation took hold. The knife blade had slit open his palm and the wound had clotted with congealed blood. He pressed it and winced, prompting Aria to finally look at him.

"You're hurt," she muttered.

Taking her flask, she poured water over the wound. He winced.

"Wait here," she said, hurrying off into the tree growth.

Jack stared at his wound, now bleeding fresh blood again, but he didn't really see it. Instead, his mind replayed the events back at the manor.

The mirror. Belle's altered fate. Aria's powers. *She's the princess.*

His mind spun and he shook his head. It was too much to take in at once. He needed time to process, but Aria had already returned. She appeared to be empty-handed but she was chewing on something, like she had found a gumball machine and got distracted on her way back.

Then she spat into her hand and rubbed a

green and brown ball of what Jack only could describe as mush between her finger and thumb.

"Give me your hand," she said.

Jack hesitated, not sure where this was going. But Aria grabbed him by the fingers and he grunted as pain shot all the way up his arm. "What are you doing?" he asked.

Aria didn't reply, but began smearing the mushy mixture onto the wound.

Jack expected it to sting, but oddly, a cooling sensation took over instead. "What *is* that?"

"A poultice. When you've lived in the woods for a year, you learn a thing or two about survival."

Jack stared at Aria in wonderment, seeing her in a new light.

"So, you're the princess…" he said carefully. "The one who The Queen is after."

Aria dropped his hand and returned to the riverbank. "I don't want to talk about it," she said, refilling the sheepskin flask.

"And you can shoot ice from your hands?" Jack pressed.

Aria huffed and turned back to him. "Listen, we need to keep moving."

Jack followed her to the horse. "Because of

the wolves. Got it," he said with a smirk. Everything was so surreal.

Aria looked at him with furrowed brows. "You think it's funny?" She stretched out her arm, showing him the genie bracelet The Queen's men had locked on her. "My powers don't work with this thing on, and without them, there's no way we would win a fight against a wolf. And had they taken this..." She gestured to the rock pendant hanging on her neck. "Even without the bracelet, my powers wouldn't be the same."

Jack wasn't trying to make light of the situation, but the thought of a powerful ice princess on the run from wolves had him tickled. Why wouldn't it? Especially after having a visit with Belle and an epic battle with The Queen's guard.

"It's just... it's like I've jumped into a fairy tale," he said finally as they climbed back on the horse.

Aria shook her head. "What the heck is a fairy tale?"

Jack laughed again.

Aria sighed. "Well, you better hold on tight. We're in for a bumpy ride."

"We go on foot from here," Aria said, tying the horse to a nearby tree. Jack's eyes narrowed at the blackened bark. *Just how much of the forest had The Queen already destroyed?* They had traveled for two days in the wintery woodland. If Aria had not given Jack her spare cloak, he would have frozen. But nothing took away the constant hunger pains. They trapped a squirrel in a snare, but it had barely enough meat to qualify as a meal. And the trees that had escaped the wrath of The Queen's inferno were deciduous. Their naked branches hovered above their heads, taunting him.

Jack's stomach growled. What he wouldn't give for a juicy red apple. At least the cuts on his hand were practically healed thanks to that mixture Aria put on it the night before.

"The swamp is just over the crest of that hill." Aria's voice snapped him from his thoughts. He followed with his jaw clenched, trying not to wince as his feet throbbed with every step.

"Of course they live in a swamp," he said through gritted teeth.

Aria turned, and her eyes flashed as she

studied him for a moment. "You're not scared, are you?"

Jack stopped and frowned at her. "No."

Aria folded her arms as if she was cold then cocked a brow, prompting Jack to finally tell her what had been plaguing his mind.

"Don't ogres… eat people? I'm just curious what the plan is here," he said, trying to sound more concerned by her lack of foresight than the thought of their impending demise. Aria pointed to the moon.

"Ogres sleep after sunset," she explained, blowing into her hands as she shivered. "We'll be in and out of there in no time."

Jack reached for her hand. It was stone-cold. "You're freezing."

She shivered again then pulled away. "Yes, well… without my powers, I become more sensitive to the cold."

"Then shouldn't we be trying to get that bracelet off?"

"No." She lifted her hands as if they were some kind of weapon. "They took my gloves, and without it… I have a hard time controlling it. It's better this way."

"Aria—"

"Enough about me. We need to get that shard." She turned on her heel and continued up the hill while Jack thought it over. Sneaking around a bunch of sleeping ogres sounded less risky than awake ogres. But he was still not entirely sold on the idea.

However, there was no turning back now.

They walked over the crest of the hill to find a snowy cave sat in the center of a marshy swamp. Jack frowned at the muddy waters, which took up much of the floor. He turned to ask Aria how to navigate the situation, but she had already darted forward.

"Aria," he hissed, going after her. He gingerly tiptoed as the ground sucked on his boots and squelched beneath his feet. He kept his eyes down, focusing all of his energy on staying upright.

Aria hissed back, "What's taking you so long?"

Jack looked up. Aria was already at the mouth of the cave. She lowered her hood and dabbed the sweat off her brow with the back of her hand. Jack picked up his pace. Mud spilled into his boots and dripped down his calves, and it was oddly soothing on his blistered feet.

"Let's make this quick, okay?"

She unsheathed a small knife and gave him a pointed look.

"Got one of those for me?" Jack whispered. Aria's brows raised as she seemed to think about it. Jack pointed at her. "Don't look at me like that. I know how to fight. I was fencing champion three years in a row, after all."

Aria rolled her eyes.

"No. I don't have another knife. So, you better keep quiet and stay close."

She hurried farther into the cave without another word. Jack followed, deep in thought. He got the impression Aria was an *act now, think later* person. But before he could brood on it more, a putrid stench of rotting eggs filled his nostrils. He covered his mouth and nose and pinched his brows as he staggered along the uneven rock floor, trying to ignore the nausea rising from his stomach.

The steep path took them deep underground, and it took all of Jack's focus not to slip on the slimy rock floor. As the ground leveled off, Jack looked up and resisted the urge to gasp. The cave opened up and moonlight poured in through cracks high above their heads.

A monstrous creature the size of a two-story

building lay face down on a nest of old rugs. Jack thought ogres were green, but this beast had waxy gray skin and a mop of dark, shaggy hair atop its head.

Aria nudged Jack and signaled for him to be quiet and keep going. Jack got the message. Now was not the time to stop and stare at the sleeping giant. They had to focus on the mission at hand.

The mirror shard.

Jack looked around. It became clear that this ogre was a hoarder. Heaps of brass ornaments littered the floor, and a large oak table riddled with woodworm sported a whole pile of clothes.

They took care to pick through the items in the cave without making any noise. If it weren't for the rotten stench, and that an ogre might wake up and devour them at any moment, Jack would have considered the steady inhale, exhale from the beast to be relaxing. He chewed his lip, searching through the stacks of books, looking for the mirror shard.

The moon offered the only source of light in the dark cave. Jack squinted and used his other senses to help him on his search. He held the objects in his soft hands and ran his fingers across every surface so not to miss anything.

Aria had done this before. She was nimble and fast, darting in and out of corners of the cave and tiptoeing back and forth like a ninja. In comparison, Jack was slow and lame. And after what seemed like hours, his search was fruitless.

"We could look through all this for weeks and never find it," Jack whispered. Aria's eyes glowed back at him. She raised a piece of glass, and the moonlight flashed in his eyes. He raised a hand to shield his face and stood up. "Is that it?"

Aria held the broken shard out and pulled out a necklace from under her clothes. But as Jack edged closer to take a better look at it, his shoe caught a jagged piece of rock. He stumbled, and in an attempt to regain his balance, he grabbed the rug on the table, taking a pile of brass plates with him as he fell.

The loud crash echoed through the cave and Jack's blood turned cold as he shakily got to his feet.

"Careful," Aria hissed as he stumbled forward. He knocked into her and the mirror shard smashed onto the floor.

Aria's eyes grew wide as she looked at him with a silent scream. "We have to move," she whispered, tugging on him. But Jack *couldn't* move.

The snoring had stopped, and the sleeping ogre sat up, staring directly at him. He pointed to it and Aria dropped his arm with a gasp.

Jack had read about ogres before. But nothing could have prepared him for the sheer magnitude of horror at being in the same space as one. And so close. The ogre's beady eyes hovered above his head, and a gaping mouth opened with an almighty roar.

This is it. We're going to die.

A strange sense of calm washed over Jack as his brain froze on the thought. Then, he said the first thing to enter his mind. "Sorry for waking you."

The ogre closed its mouth and stared at Jack like he was from outer space.

"Run!" Aria grabbed Jack's arm and they dashed for the mouth of the cave, but the ogre was faster. Two thunderous strides had him standing right where they needed to go.

"I like a midnight snack," he said. The vapors of his breath could be a weapon in themselves. The stench had Jack's stomach rolling again. He was just about to apologize to Aria for waking the ogre and getting them in this mess, but she had already leapt into action. With a flick of the wrist, something sailed across the cave, and the next moment the ogre howled. Jack looked away from Aria's triumphant face to see the ogre had fallen to his knees with a thud, cradling his face.

"I can't see. You nasty little vermin. Who do you think you are?" the ogre roared. He slammed his fists against the wall of the cave and rocks plummeted from above. "Wait till I get my hands on you. I'll crush your bones and gobble you up whole."

The ogre's good eye swiveled left and right before it settled on Jack and a sickening grin invaded his face. With a snort, he stepped forward and reached for Jack, but Jack lunged to the side, narrowly avoiding the ogre's grasp.

Aria raised her bow and aimed at the ogre. Just as he took another swipe, the arrow sailed through the air and landed in the ogre's good eye. The monster howled and stomped his feet, prompting the ground to tremble beneath their feet like an earthquake. Now that the ogre was truly blind, they had a chance to escape.

Only, one problem: the wounded ogre was still blocking their only exit. Suddenly, Jack was struck by an idea.

"I am sorry you are hurt," Jack said calmly. "I

take it you are a collector. Tell me, do you like to collect knowledge too?"

The ogre stopped moving.

"What kind of knowledge?" he asked.

"How about a name so secret, you'd be the only living creature to know it?" Jack suggested. Aria shot him a look, her eyes widening.

"What is this secret name?" the ogre grumbled. Jack took a few steps forward, confident he'd piqued the ogre's curiosity, that he was not going to be dinner.

"The name of your attacker that is. The most wanted thief in the whole forest—" He glanced back at a horrified Aria, who had lowered her bow and stared at him like he was a traitor. He turned back to the ogre. "Is that a name you want to know?"

The ogre thought about it and mumbled something inaudible. Then, he lowered his hands a fraction. Aria raised her bow again and aimed.

"The name is *no one*," Jack said firmly. The ogre was quiet for a moment, contemplating this lie. Then he growled, and the shift in the air had Jack on alert. He narrowly missed a swipe from the ogre, who clawed the air with fingers like boulders, desperate to grasp his attackers. He roared with so much ferocity, it sent chills down Jack's spine.

Aria and Jack darted side to side, evading his clutches. Frustrated and annoyed, the ogre roared again, a rancid smell like gas in a hot furnace filled the cave.

"Brother? Are you being attacked?" The distant roars from outside of the cave made Jack and Aria exchange looks. How could they deal with more of them? And did she even get her knife back?

"Brothers! No one is here!" the ogre cried out, staggering farther down the cave. Jack and Aria pressed against the edges, hiding behind the rocks and careful not to make a sound.

"Then who is attacking you?" another ogre asked.

"No one is attacking me!"

The ogres stomped away, causing the ground to tremor.

"Go back to sleep, you daft old cod."

The blinded ogre moaned out of frustration but turned around and headed for Jack and Aria. They hurried back into the cave and hid in a pile of rugs, daring not to breathe, as the ogre felt his way back to bed.

"Are you still here?" he asked. "No one. Is no one here?"

Aria reached for another arrow, ready to finish the ogre off, but Jack touched her hand and shook his head at her. Why was killing her first instinct? The ogre crashed back onto his bed of rugs and rolled over, turning his back to them. Snoring soon followed, with intermittent whimpering.

Now was their chance. Without hesitation, the two of them crept out from their hiding place. As they hurried for the mouth of the cave, Aria picked up her knife from the ground and wiped the blade on her cloak before sheathing it again.

"I can't believe what just happened," she said as they reentered the swamp. Jack took greedy gulps of fresh air, relieved to be out of the cave. "That was clever, calling me 'no one.'" She looked at him as if she was only seeing him for the first time. "I thought you were going to sell me out and make a run for it."

Jack touched her arm and gave it a light squeeze. "I would never do that."

They walked in silence across the boggy floor, reeling from their narrow escape.

"It was like you knew the other ogres would

come over," Aria said, scratching her wrist thoughtfully.

Jack grinned.

"I can't take all the credit. You've got Homer to thank for that trick."

Aria gave him a puzzled look. "Who?"

Jack cocked a brow at her. "*The Odyssey*? Come on, that's a classic. What kind of books do you have in this world?"

Aria looked at him blankly and shrugged.

"I give up," Jack said with a sigh.

He took another step and something cracked beneath his foot. Then a net sprung from the ground and bundled Aria and Jack together as it swung in the air beneath a tree.

"Was this part of the story, too?" Aria asked, taking out her knife.

"No."

The rope creaked above their heads and Aria wasted no time, already cutting the net with her knife. But heavy footsteps announced the return of the ogres, and Aria stopped. Her eyes glued to Jack with a mixture of disbelief and regret.

"Well, what do we have here?" A giant ogre's face appeared, his eye pressed up close to the net. He flicked the net with his finger, sending them swinging towards the tree trunk, and Aria dropped her knife.

"Monty, stop that. Didn't Mama teach us not to play with our food?"

The net tightened, pushing Aria's body up against Jack. She leaned into him, letting out a long, defeated breath. Jack couldn't remember the last time he had been so close to a girl. Or anyone, for that matter.

He hugged her back and squeezed, taken by how natural it was to have her in his arms.

"It's okay. We're going to get out of this, I prom—" Before he could finish, the rope snapped and the two of them crashed to the ground. Jack hit his head on a rock as roars echoed in his ears. Aria's scream was the last sound he heard before he drifted into nothingness.

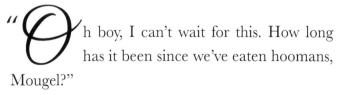

"*O*h boy, I can't wait for this. How long has it been since we've eaten hoomans, Mougel?"

"*Humans*, you fried turnip!"

"Manny, get over here. Tell us why you lied to your brothers."

"I was telling no lies."

"There it is again. Lies. You said no one was here. You wanted to eat the hoomans all for yourself, didn't you?"

"Greedy Manny. Now look at you."

"I'm not lying!"

Jack blinked as his eyes adjusted to the darkness. His nose hovered an inch above the boggy ground and his hands and feet were tied to something. He cocked his head and saw that it was a piece of log.

"Help me light the fire, Monty."

Aria was tied next to him in the same downward position, and his heart sank when he realized what was about to happen.

"Got any ideas?" she murmured quietly.

"Not exactly," he said.

Three giant ogres sat together, fumbling with boulders that were like pebbles in their hands, attempting to start a fire. But despite their clumsiness, the kindling sparked and set alight. Jack's forehead perspired as he wrestled to free himself from his bonds, but his legs and hands were tied so tightly, his efforts were fruitless.

"Well, it was nice knowing you, Jack," Aria said glumly as the ogres stoked the fire with a branch. The orange flames danced in the air and Jack's stomach knotted.

"I never pegged you as one to give up," he muttered, straining his grip, still trying to loosen the rope.

"I guess being killed by them is better than by The Queen."

"Time to cook the hoomans."

The announcement was greeted by the most unexpected sound: angry roars and cries. But they were coming from the ogres. They gnashed their teeth and stomped the ground ferociously, but Jack couldn't see what was happening.

Until a pair of boots appeared under Jack's nose.

"I can't believe it," Aria said. A rough pair of hands grasped the rope and began to cut them free. Moments later, Aria hopped down and threw her arms around their rescuer. Jack's feet, now free from their bonds, fell to the floor and he wriggled his hands out of the loose rope.

"Nice to see you again, Princess."

He knew she was the princess? I thought she kept her identity a secret?

Jack stood up and looked at a tall, slender young man with dirty blonde hair. He could not

have been older than twenty-five. He had a stub-
bled chin, deep-set eyes and a wicked grin as he
looked at Aria like an old friend. A finely carved
bow sat on his shoulder and he carried a sword
painted in blood.

A group of men chased off the last ogre, then
celebrated by the fire with a dance.

"Robin, you don't know how glad I am to see
you," Aria said, her face flushed with color. He
patted her on the shoulder with a gentle look.

"I'm glad we weren't too late," he said,
nodding to his friends by the fire. "Why don't you
warm up and say hi to the boys. They've missed
you."

Aria took off with a run to greet her old
friends, picking up her knife on the way. Jack
watched her, still stunned by the unexpected turn
of events. Just seconds ago he was certain they
were going to be ogre food. He turned to Robin
Hood and offered his hand.

"Robin Hood. Thank you for—"

He didn't finish because in a flash, Robin's
face darkened and he took out his bow, aiming an
arrow right between Jack's eyes.

"I'm going to kill you for what you've done."

ARIA

$\mathcal{A}$ria curled up in the corner of a stable and hugged her legs, shivering. She could have unlocked them out of Robin's makeshift cell if she wasn't so drained of energy. But she hadn't had a decent rest since she sold Jack to Ryke, so she decided to lean her head against the rocky wall and close her eyes. Though, even if she did want to help Jack, she could barely move. She wasn't used to being cold, and it didn't help that the temperature was only getting colder as the night went on.

"I don't suppose you know how to pick a lock, do you?" Jack asked, and she didn't have to open her eyes to know he was shoving a stick into the lock. It snapped in two, prompting Jack to grumble something inaudible.

"Relax," Aria muttered. "He thinks you're The Intruder. Once we explain that you're not, he'll let us go. You should get some rest."

"Easy for you to say," Jack murmured, throwing the broken stick aside as if it had betrayed him. "He doesn't want your head on a plate."

Aria chuckled at how dramatic he was sometimes. "He's not gonna hurt you."

"Really? It didn't look like that when he had an arrow hovering an inch away from my brain. How can you be so sure?"

"Because I know him. And this is what he does. He tells you he's going to kill you, then locks you up to agonize enough so that when he comes back, you're ready to tell him everything he wants to know. Classic Robin move."

"That's awful. Why did he lock *you* up, anyway?" Jack asked, sitting across from her. "I thought you two were friends?"

"We are." She let out a long breath. "He sent me in here to convince you to tell him about The Intruder. But since you don't know anything about him, I'm going to get some rest."

"Why did you leave?"

"The Queen found out he had taken me in and burned down his village during the night. His parents are dead because of me." Aria shivered again, but it wasn't just the cold this time. A wave of regret washed over her. But when she opened her eyes, Jack was at her side, removing his cloak and throwing it over her shoulders.

"What about you?" she asked, almost stuttering as her teeth chattered.

"I feel fine. You look frozen," he said, sitting next to her. "Would you like me to try to get that genie bracelet off of you?"

"You can't even pick a lock," she teased, but when the cold rushed to her head, she became serious. "It's not safe. Without my gloves, it's harder to control my powers."

Jack wrapped his arms around her, and she gave him a quizzical look.

"What are you doing?"

"Keeping you from getting hypothermia," he said, ignoring her reluctance and pulling her into him.

As soon as she pressed against his chest, an unexpected wave of heat washed over her. It was as if she were sitting in front of a fire, and before her brain could process anything else, she melted into his arms.

Oh, the warmth radiating from him was just what she needed. But what caught her mostly by surprise was how natural it felt being in his arms. She focused on the slow rhythm of his breathing. She couldn't think of anything more soothing.

"Is that better?" he asked, his voice gentle in her ear. When the warmth of his breath brushed her cheek, she buried her face in his chest.

"Much better," she whispered.

"So, why isn't it safe to take this thing off?" he asked, running his thumb over the metal. Aria found herself wondering how his touch would've felt against her skin instead, but then shook her head and focused on the bracelet.

"The longer my body goes without releasing power, the stronger the urge becomes," she explained, turning her wrist. "And I can feel it. As soon as I get my powers back, it's going to burst out of me. I won't be able to contain it." She bit her lip against the bubble of emotion rising in her chest. As the force of her powers intensified, her ability to shut off her emotions weakened.

"If you're stronger than The Queen, why don't you fight back?" Jack asked.

Aria let out a defeated breath. "Because if I lose and fall under her control... she'll turn me into a weapon. Not that I can blame her. She has every reason to hate me."

"Why is that?"

Aria's heart ached at the memory. "Because she believes I killed her son."

"Did you?"

A few seconds passed. "Yes."

She was expecting Jack to loosen his embrace, but he didn't. "Well, I'm sure you had a good reason."

She pulled back and studied his face, scanning for any sign of sarcasm, but found only kindness. Anyone else would've thought of her as a monster, but his gentle nature was endearing. He reminded her so much of her sister. "How can you be so trusting?" she asked.

"Because you didn't have to come back for me," he said, pushing a strand of her brown hair from her face. "And because I have a feeling the only reason you don't want to fight The Queen is because you don't want to kill her." He held her gaze for a long time, and something in the pit of her stomach fluttered. "Caring for people isn't a weakness, Aria. It makes you stronger. That's why

I'm certain you will learn to control your abilities."

Aria stared into his blue eyes, his words stirring up intense feelings like a whirlwind. The confidence in his voice infused her with more hope than she ever thought possible. She glanced at his lips, and a strong urge to kiss him flooded her.

No.

She ripped herself from his arms, and the freezing cold whiplashed her body almost instantly. "How can you possibly know that?" she snapped, jumping to her feet and moving away from him.

"Because I can feel it," he said, calmly standing. But before he could follow her, she turned to him with a glare.

"You know my story too, don't you?" She wanted to be angry with him. Anger was safer than all the other emotions swirling inside. Forbidden emotions. And for that, she needed to push him away, to put as much distance between them as possible. "You've been manipulating me this whole time."

"No, I haven't." He lifted his palms defensively as she clenched her fists. How could she have dropped her guard with him? "I never read about you, I swear."

"Robin!" she yelled, turning toward the iron bars. She needed to get away from Jack, or there was no telling what temptations she would succumb to. "Robin!"

"Aria!" a young woman's voice called out from across the cave. Her red hood shone in the faint moonlight.

"Ry! Thank goodness." Aria let out a sigh of relief, her breath thick in the cold air. "Tell Robin to quit playing around and get us out of here."

"He's not playing around," Ry replied, her expression serious as she pulled out a set of keys from under her hood and looked for the right one. "He really does want The Intruder dead, and I have never seen him so determined."

"Why?" Jack asked, approaching the bars.

His warmth enveloped Aria, and she thought about curling up in his arms again. Then she stepped away from him in an attempt to clear her head. *What's getting into me?*

"Open the flipping door!" Aria barked, snatching the keys from Ry's hands. She didn't like snapping at Ry, they were friends, but she could no longer control her irritation. And her mind needed a distraction from the whirlwind of emotions that kept wanting to overtake her just like her powers did.

"I think it's this one," Aria mumbled, placing the key into the lock. When it clicked, she charged out of the cell. "Robin!"

"Aria, wait." Ry grabbed Aria's arm, stopping her. "Maybe it's best if you just take The Intruder and go. Your horse is outside."

"Jack—" Saying his name made her chest ache with a yearning she'd never had before, and she clenched her jaw. "*He...* is not The Intruder. And you and I both know that Robin will track us wherever we go."

Ry didn't deny it. Robin was stellar at the chase game. Especially with his merry men. But unlike Aria, Ry was always one to bet on the impossible. It was more than just hope. She believed in chances. Some may even call it *miracles*.

"What did The Intruder do to him?" Jack asked, his voice low and pensive behind Aria.

His voice gave her butterflies. She pressed her eyes shut, keeping her emotions at bay. Why was the pull toward Jack so strong?

That was when her eyes landed on the bracelet. Her body was already in overload, fighting against her suppressed powers. Now, her emotions were spiraling out of control.

This is just a side effect from the bracelet. It's not real.

Aria yanked her arm from Ry's grip and stomped out of the stables. Her heart sank as she looked around the half-built buildings. Robin had taken them back to his village. They seemed to be rebuilding it.

She walked across the deserted village to what looked like the square. Though it was empty, she recognized the small well in the center, surrounded by the remains of what used to be shops and homes.

"Robin!" she yelled, her voice echoing in the night. "Show yourself."

"So bossy," he responded from a rooftop. "You can get the girl out of the castle, but you can't take the princess out of the girl."

"What do you want?" she asked.

"I want The Intruder to die," he said simply, no anger or pain or sadness in his voice. He was simply stating a fact. But Aria would need more than that.

"What did he do to you?"

"Me?" Robin chuckled, adjusting the quiver

strapped to his back. "He didn't just ruin me. He ruined everyone's fate."

That wasn't news to Aria. She'd heard about The Intruder from Belle, and she was very much aware of the mess he'd made, but none of that was Jack's fault. "Well, Jack isn't the person you're looking for."

"He came from the same mirror, did he not?" Robin asked, and as much as Aria wanted to deny it, she couldn't. She bit her lip. Robin had eyes and ears in the whole forest. Of course he knew about Jack's arrival. Robin was good at reading people. "Then who's to say he won't rumple people's lives all over again?"

"He's been with me since the moment he arrived," Aria assured him. "He's not The Intruder, and he's done nothing wrong."

"Not yet."

Aria stepped in front of Jack, who had slowly made his way toward her. Ry stood far off, watching.

"I won't let you hurt him," Aria said firmly, clenching her fists.

"Oh, I won't be hurting him," Robin said, pulling out an arrow and nocking it on his bow. "You will."

He loosed the arrow, and with his flawless aim, it hit the small hinge on Aria's bracelet. The metal fell on the snow with a soft thud, but the release of power that erupted from Aria's hands was like a bolt of lightning.

Jack dropped to the ground as ice spewed from her palms, freezing everything in its path. The whirlwind she had inside transformed into a howling blizzard that circled the square. The blackened trees turned white, as did the forest as far as the eye could see.

When her eyes landed on Jack, who was still on the ground, she balled her hands into fists before the ice could shoot at him. But suppressing her powers was like trying to hold back an earthquake, and her body trembled.

She dropped to her knees in front of him, her veins bulging as her muscles strained. And when their eyes met, she saw her reflection in them. Hers had already turned gray, and she was running out of time. The moment they become white, she would be blinded and lose all control.

"Run," she spoke through gritted teeth, but when Jack didn't move, she realized there was nowhere he could go. She had frozen them into an ice dome.

"No!" She punched the ground, sending a frozen shockwave through the snow until there was nothing but ice.

Aria shoved her closed fists into her cloak then curled into a ball. She rocked back and forth, barely able to breathe. Keeping the raging force of her powers from devastating everything around her was impossible. But she knew that the second she let go, her powers would hit Jack with an immense force and he would never survive the impact.

"You can control it." Jack's voice landed softly in her ears, the warmth of his breath brushing her cheek.

"I can't," she said, almost apologetic. "You need to get away from me. I don't want to hurt you."

"You *won't* hurt me," he said firmly, and she looked up to meet his eyes.

"You don't know that."

"I can feel it," he insisted. "Let me show you."

"Jack, don't—"

"Do you trust me?" he asked.

With eyes full of tears, she nodded.

He reached around her neck and removed her necklace. She gasped as a sudden wave of relief washed over her, fueling her soul with a strange sense of control.

"Your powers are strong," he whispered, touching her shoulder. "But your heart is stronger."

She sucked in a deep breath as the weight of a thousand seas lifted from her shoulders. By the time her unclenched fists dropped to her sides, the howling blizzard had faded and the ice dome melted, creating a puddle of water around them. But they were too engrossed in each other to even notice how drenched they had become.

"How did you know that would work?" she whispered, out of breath, her heart still racing.

Jack smiled, his hand still pressed against her skin. "I didn't. But I trusted you."

"Why?" Her muscles throbbed. "Why are you so sure of me?"

"Because…" He held her gaze for a long time as if contemplating whether or not to tell her a secret. "I saw you," he finally said. "At the cemetery. And in the mirror, before I fell in. You were the person I saw. You drew me here. And now it's all starting to make sense…" He cupped her face with his warm hands and peered deeper into her eyes. "I don't know how or why, but I don't think me coming here was an accident."

Aria had no idea what Jack was talking about, but her heart soared at the thought of having pulled him into her life. How was that possible? And for what? They could never be together.

Aria spotted a swift movement from her peripheral vision, and in the blink of an eye, she stretched out her hand, shooting a wave of frozen crystals at Robin, pinning him to a wall of ice.

"Hold that thought," she said, pulling away from Jack's affection only to turn toward Robin with the darkest glare.

Robin didn't seem fearful as Aria marched toward him, balls of ice forming above her open palms. It was as if he no longer cared whether he lived or died.

Aria stood in front of him with eyes like that of an angry wolf. "Give me one good reason why I shouldn't freeze your heart and shatter it into pieces."

"Go on," he said, his voice void of all emotion. "As you wish."

"Aria, wait!" Ry yelled, running toward them. "Please, don't do it."

"I'm sorry, Ry." Aria shifted her glare back to Robin. "But there is no excuse for what he just did."

"Robin, just tell her," Ry pleaded, but Robin didn't move a muscle. Not that he could with how much ice Aria had thrown at him. "Fine, then I will."

"Ry, don't." Finally, there was some emotion in Robin's voice as he watched his cousin grab his quiver from the ground and turn it upside down. His arrows clattered to the ground, along with a piece of parchment.

Ry threw the quiver aside and picked up the paper from the snow-covered ground. "Here…" She handed it to Aria.

She unfolded the paper and Jack came to stand at her side. "What is this?" Aria asked.

"It's a page from his book," Jack muttered, taking the paper from Aria to examine it further. "Where did you get this?"

"So, you *do* know our fate," Robin spat out.

Jack looked up from the page to meet Robin's glare. "Back in my world, I read a story about you… your past. But here, everything is different."

"Not everything," Robin hissed.

"What is that supposed to mean?" Aria asked, turning to look at Robin again.

"The wolf's got Marian." Robin said her name as if it left a bitter taste in his mouth. "And I shouldn't care since she's engaged to be married to that stupid king. But since that cursed page appeared in my quiver, I can't get her out of my head!"

"That's because she's your true love," Jack explained, looking at Robin. "She's your happy ending. Or at least, she was supposed to be."

"It's not too late," Ry chimed in, turning to look at her cousin, who was still pinned to the wall by ice. "You just need to save her."

"I can't."

"Why not?" Aria asked.

"Because I'm the one who delivered her to the wolf," Robin said.

"Why did you do that?" Jack asked.

"Because he was offering a nice reward," Robin said, looking around the square. "And we need money to rebuild the village."

Aria turned to Robin again. "It still doesn't explain why you did what you did... to *me*."

Robin softened his gaze, and for the first time

that night he resembled the friend who had taken her in and trained her as a little sister.

"You are stronger than you know," he said, looking her in the eyes. "You need to stop running away and fight for your kingdom before she kills us all."

"And how would killing Jack accomplish that?" she asked.

Robin shrugged. "I figured that would just be an added bonus."

Another ball of ice formed over Aria's open hand. But then Jack touched her shoulder, and a wave of warmth washed over her, filling her with a sense of calm.

"Let him go," Jack said.

The ball of ice kept spinning over her palm. "Not until he promises he won't lay a hand on you."

"I promise," Robin said.

"Or an *arrow*," Jack added, and Robin rolled his eyes.

"Fine, if you want to take away all my fun," he grumbled. "I promise. Now, get this thing off of me before I lose a limb from frostbite."

At the turn of Aria's finger, the ice block

melted, and Robin was finally free. She then leaned against Jack's warm chest.

"So, now what?" Ry asked, watching as her cousin picked up his arrows from the ground and placed them back into his quiver.

"Now, we go get Miriam back." Once Robin had his quiver safely strapped to his back, he looked at Aria. "We could use the help."

"We can't," she said, her voice tired more than anything. "We need to go find the rest of the shards." She left out the fact that this was so she and Jack could leave that realm and never look back.

"Which shard are you referring to?" Robin asked, curious.

"The Mirror of Reason," Aria explained. "We had stolen a shard from the ogres, but… we lost it."

"Not the right one, you didn't." Robin reached into his own satchel and pulled out a crimson cloth, and Aria's eyes widened.

"Is that…?"

Robin nodded, handing it to her. "We stole it from the ogres a while back and switched it with a dummy one."

Aria unwrapped the cloth until she could see her reflection in the mirror. Her blonde hair shimmered in the bright light of the moon. She wrapped it up quickly before anyone could see how much of her reflection changed. The Mirror of Reason was known to show the purest form of a human.

"Thank you," she muttered to Robin while handing the cloth to Jack since her satchel was still in the stables.

Robin stood in front of her, then placed a rough hand on her shoulder. "You know I wouldn't be so tough on you if I didn't think you could handle it, right?"

She nodded, and he gave her shoulder a light squeeze. But when he turned to Jack, Aria braced herself to tackle him to the ground if he even *thought* of breaking his promise.

"Take care of her," Robin said, slapping Jack on the shoulder before walking away.

Aria let out a relieved breath then leaned her back into Jack's chest.

"Where to from here?" he asked, wrapping his arms around her while still holding the shard.

Aria closed her tired eyes. "My hiding place."

JACK

*J*ack couldn't sleep. He glanced at Aria's sleeping figure, her back slowly rising and falling, before looking at the silver bracelet in his hands. Despite its delicate design, it was heavy. Like chainmail. How could a piece of jewelry control Aria's powers? Sure, it was a fairy-tale land, but there had to be an explanation. And the mystery behind it intrigued him.

Aria's place was a burrow underneath a huge tree, hidden deep in the woods. The sun had risen by the time they reached it, and Aria crawled into a bed in the corner and promptly fell asleep. But Jack had so many questions.

Who was The Intruder, and where did he

come from? Was the mirror a portal to other lands, or just England? If everyone in the Chanted Forest was a character in the fairy tale books, who was Aria? Was her happy ending messed up too? And who was the pirate who captured him? How did he even know who Jack was?

Jack looked up at the sound of Aria talking in her sleep. He chewed his lip, conflicted as he debated if he should get a better listen. Part of him wanted to respect her privacy, but if he was to keep putting his life in her hands, he needed to know more about her.

Back in the stables, he had thought things were going well, considering the unfortunate circumstance. She even let him hold her, which he'd been longing to do again ever since. But her reaction to his affection was very unexpected. At first, he thought it was because she didn't like being vulnerable, but then she became almost panicked. That was when he realized there was more she wasn't letting on. And it wasn't just her inability to control her powers.

Aria mumbled again, and Jack craned his neck, trying to understand her soft murmur.

"George…" Her whisper was light as a

feather, but it landed on Jack's ears like a thunder-storm. She was dreaming of George. *Who the heck is George?* Could that have been the reason she kept pushing Jack away?

The burrow was dark with only a few weak beams of morning light peeping in through thick undergrowth, and the woody scent made his throat dry.

Jack frowned as he rubbed his neck and set the bracelet down. With so many unanswered ques-tions, he pulled out one of the mirror shards from the crimson cloth and lifted it to his eyes, as if this magical mirror might solve all of life's mysteries. As he shifted closer to the faint light, he glimpsed his reflection.

"What are you doing?"

Jack jumped and almost dropped the shard. He fumbled with it and set it down as he looked up at Aria. Her eyes were like slits and her face broke into a yawn. For the first time, Jack had a wave of sleepiness wash over him as he yawned back.

"I was just looking…" He didn't even know what he was looking for. "I'm sorry to wake you. Go back to sleep." *Back to dreaming about George*, he wanted to add.

"Are you okay?" she asked.

Jack shrugged. "Just tired, I guess."

"Then you should get some sleep," she said, moving toward him and taking both shards from his hands. "I'll put these away." She stared at them longingly, and her soft expression made Jack wonder whether she was really running away from The Queen, or if her plan was to go wherever this George guy was. "Hey…" She flashed him a soft smile. "Wanna see the mirror?"

Jack's eyes widened. "It's here?"

She stood, and Jack scrambled to his feet, following her further into the burrow until she stopped in front of a wall of ice. Aria waved a hand in the air and the ice evaporated, revealing a large oval mirror propped up against the wall. He inspected the elaborate designs on the brass frame.

"These markings… I recognize them from the mirror in my grandfather's study," Jack said, tracing the foreign language etched into the frame with his index finger.

"It's Elven," Aria said, setting the two shards in place. She hovered her fingertip over the joins and sealed the glass in place with ice.

Jack's brows rose. "You mean, like... elves?"

Aria gave him a puzzled frown. "You don't have elves where you're from?"

Jack shook his head. "No, we're all pretty normal where I'm from. Nobody has powers or pointy ears."

Aria studied the mirror, deep in thought. Jack liked seeing that thoughtful expression on her face. It was better than her glare or scowl. Or worse, sorrow.

"Sounds boring," she said after a long silence.

Jack shrugged with a smirk. Compared to the Chanted Forest, Oxford was entirely dull. Tyneham even more so. He had been on more adventures in the last week than he had his entire life at the manor. But he still needed to go back. His entire life was there.

He shook the thoughts out of his mind and watched Aria staring in silence, chewing her lip. A strand of dark hair obscured her cheek, and Jack longed to sweep it aside. But he resisted. Last time they got close on their own, she freaked out and practically ran away from him.

His thoughts replayed the events at the village. The ice dome, the flurries of snowflakes dancing around them, forming frozen spheres. How the winds threw her hair back and her eyes turned gray. She was a force of nature—or something completely *unnatural*.

"This mirror is beyond anything I've ever seen," she whispered, still deep in her own thoughts, but by thinking aloud, it was as if she was inviting Jack into them. He listened attentively as she continued. The corner of her lips lifted a little. "They should've called it the Mirror B*eyond* Reason." She chuckled at her own joke, and Jack found himself smiling with her. "Want to see something interesting?"

Jack arched a brow. "Sure."

She turned the mirror toward him, and Jack followed her line of sight. Her reflection looked back, only the girl in the mirror had ash blonde hair.

"Aria," he said, finally breaking out of his thoughts. She didn't respond. She just looked at him, her round eyes blue as a summer's day once more as she waited for him to process what he was seeing. "Your hair…"

Aria's eyes glistened. "I dyed my hair so The Queen won't find me so easily."

"That's right. You were blonde when I first saw you. Why don't I look any different?" Jack glanced at himself with a slight smirk. This was the first time he had seen himself in the clothes Belle had given him. He looked like a prince— although a bit disheveled.

"I never showed anyone that before," Aria said, looking away as she bit her lip.

"Then why share it with me?" he asked, genuinely curious.

It took her a few seconds to answer, but to Jack they were the longest seconds of his life. "I'm just tired of hiding the real me."

She turned around and met his eyes for the first time since they left the village, and Jack broke into a smile. He reached out to cradle her cheek. Just as his fingertips reached her face, she jumped back, leaving Jack with his hand frozen mid-air.

"Okay. Now I'm really confused."

"It's best if you don't touch me," she said, backing away from him and rushing to a small bundle of clothes. She rummaged around and pulled out another pair of gloves.

When she said nothing else, he let out a tired sigh then gave her a pointed look. "Is this about George?"

Aria's eyes widened in shock. "What?"

"Is he the reason you keep pushing me away?"

"How do you even know about him?" she asked, her face twisting in confusion.

"You said his name in your sleep," Jack confessed, surprised at the tightness in his chest. "So, who is he?"

Aria paced the room with a deep sigh. "It doesn't even matter."

Jack watched her as he brushed off his pant legs. "If you're calling out to him in your sleep, I'm pretty sure he matters."

Aria shook her head. "It doesn't matter because he's dead."

"Oh." Jack wasn't entirely sure how to respond. "I'm sorry. Did The Queen kill him too?"

"No." Aria stopped and looked at him, her face softening. "I did."

The words hung in the air and made Jack's ears ring. It was the last thing he expected Aria to say, and for a moment he stood frozen and stared at her with disbelief.

"Was he The Queen's son?" Jack asked, connecting the dots in his head.

"Yes," Aria admitted. "But I didn't mean to kill him. George was my best friend." A small smile formed on her lips as her eyes became distant. "We grew up together, even before my sister came along. He was like a brother to me." But then her smile faded and her eyes darkened. "He was nothing like his mother. He was sweet and loyal."

Aria stopped talking and looked down. Jack's stomach churned. "What happened?"

Aria huffed, dragging her fingers through her hair with frustration. "He kissed me. That's all it took for him to turn into a sculpture of ice."

Aria looked away in shame, and Jack took a step forward, wanting to wrap her in his arms and comfort her like he had in the cell, but he hesitated. He wondered if he, too, would turn to ice if he got too close.

"Couldn't you just melt the ice?" he asked, curious.

"I tried, but I must've frozen him from inside out," she said, pacing the room again. "The Queen accused me of having planned that all along, but I would never have caused him harm." She turned to look at Jack again, and he could see the honesty in her eyes. "Even though I wasn't in love with him, I did care for him. Deeply."

Jack nodded, assuring her that he believed her.

"That's how the war got started, and because of me, my family is dead. My parents, my sweet, gentle sister… you remind me of her. She used to treat the servants like friends and she'd sneak extra food out of the kitchen and give it to the maids. She was so kind and selfless, yet because of me… she's gone," she whispered, looking up to meet his eyes. He stood close to her, and for the first time, she didn't recoil from his touch.

"You are not responsible for their deaths," he said softly.

Aria buried her face in his chest, and he instinctively wrapped his arms around her, his thoughts in high gear. The burnt trees, destroyed villages. So much death and destruction to get her hands on Aria. All because, what? So she could terrorize people with Aria's powers?

"We need to find the final shard," Aria said, pulling away again. "The sooner I'm gone, the safer for everyone."

Jack wasn't sure how running away would solve anything. The Queen would surely burn the whole kingdom to the ground. But he didn't argue. At least if they found the last shard and repaired the mirror, they could come up with a plan. Without it, they had nothing.

"Right. So, this was made by elves?" Jack asked, turning serious as he approached the mirror. Aria joined him, her shoulders relaxing as the air became light again.

"Yes, it is said that the elves have an understanding of the elements far better than any living creature. They craft the best weapons. My knife for example—" She unsheathed her knife and held it out for Jack to look. The blade glittered in the weak sunlight. "It can pierce through a dragon's scale."

"Did they make this too?" Jack picked up the silver bracelet from the ground and held it out for Aria. But she took a step back as if it were kryptonite.

"Why did you bring that?" she asked, almost offended.

"You really think it would be a good idea to leave something like this lying around?" Upon seeing Aria's unimpressed frown, Jack stuffed it in his pocket. "You won't see it again, I promise."

When something shiny caught Jack's eye, he squinted into the mirror. He then looked back over his shoulder to confirm that what he was seeing wasn't actually in the burrow, but only in the mirror.

"What are you doing?" Aria asked, looking at him with puzzlement.

"Do you see that?" Jack edged forward and pointed into the mirror again. A brown chest with a shiny brass lock sat afar off. Aria turned around then gasped and hovered an inch away from the glass.

"Oh my heck! The mirror is showing us where the final shard is," she said with an excited squeal.

"And where is that?" Jack scratched his head.

"There is only one place I know that would have a treasure chest." Aria beamed at Jack, her eyes sparkling. "Pirate Cove."

Jack inwardly groaned. *Pirates?* Suddenly his adrenaline faded and exhaustion took over. The last thing he wanted to do was to go off and steal from a bunch of pirates. Aria studied his face as if his thoughts were written on his forehead.

"Do you still have my necklace?" she asked, stretching out her hand.

Jack dropped it in her open palm, and she put around her neck.

"You need to rest. If you think it's been fun so far," she said, placing her small hand on his tense shoulder. "Just wait and see what's in store for us tomorrow."

*P*irate Cove was a full day's walk, and the forest was eerily quiet. They did not cross paths with another living soul, much to Jack's relief. Even after a full day and night's rest, he didn't know how much more drama he could handle.

Aria explained that Pirate Cove was on a small island just off the northern coast. The island was surrounded by jagged rocks and thrashing waters. When Jack asked how they could possibly cross such a treacherous passage, Aria just looked at him blankly.

Oh, how convenient it must be to have powers.

"We're close."

The horse slowed and they jumped down. Aria took confident strides to a nearby tree and fastened the reins. As Jack dismounted the horse, he noticed the dull ache in his hands had gone. He inspected his palm to see his wound had already scarred. *That poultice might be gross, but it was effective,* he thought. Aria was busying herself with the reins while Jack swaggered like a cowboy, tugging on his pant legs with a disgruntled groan.

Walking on solid ground after riding a horse all day was unnatural.

He was just about to grumble about his inner thighs burning when a commotion broke out in the distance. Aria whipped around, her knife out and her eyes darting around them. She met Jack's shocked stare and raised a finger to her lips.

He nodded and the two of them crept in the direction of the noise. An unearthly sound ricocheted around them, mingled with shouting and waves crashing onto land. There was a succession of huge splashes, and Jack had visions of dolphins leaping in and out of the water.

"Come on," Aria whispered. They stooped low to avoid a branch and darted into the tree line. They had come far enough to find woodland not yet scorched by The Queen. The frosted leaves rustled under their feet and when Jack stepped on a twig, the crack sent blood rushing to his face. But the shouts and screeches were too loud for anyone to notice, except for Aria who shot him a look as she grabbed his arm and yanked him down to crouch with her.

They peered through the bare branches. Jack squinted against the spray of icy cold mist and rubbed his eyes.

"What the—"

Aria pulled him with her and he stumbled forward, trying to keep up. Running onto the beach during all the commotion was not something Jack would have thought of doing. But Aria didn't even hesitate. She pulled off her gloves and stretched out her arms as they slowed to a stop.

A magnificent pirate ship bobbed in the distance with its black flags waving as the ship rocked. An iridescent fin emerged from the water and disappeared with a splash. Jack rubbed his eyes in disbelief and looked again. Pirates thrashed in the water as dazzling women circled them like beautiful sharks. He swallowed as his brain processed what they were.

Mermaids.

They had long flowing hair, golden skin, and a smile that took Jack's breath away. He watched as the pirates walked peacefully into the water, mesmerized by the creatures in awe. Only to be snatched and pulled under.

One by one, the mermaids grasped a pirate and flung them against the jagged rocks. And just like that, Jack snapped out of his trance.

Aria threw her hands out and blasts of ice shot out in frozen fractals. The white water thrashed against giant black rocks and more than a dozen pirates cried out in the water, their arms flailing as they tried to swim away from their alluring attackers.

"What are you waiting for? Come on." Aria nudged Jack and ran. In the moments Jack had been watching the pirates fighting with the mermaids in the perilous seas, Aria had fashioned an uneven ice path to the island.

Aria looked at her hands as if impressed with the control of power she'd just displayed. The bridge of ice she built looked steady enough, but given her history with her powers being unreliable, he studied the structure hesitantly.

"Are you sure this will hold?" he asked, stepping onto the frozen plank. Aria dashed forward, her dark hair and cloak billowing out behind her.

Jack's heart thumped wildly in his chest as he followed after her, skating his feet across the ice. He tried to stop his imagination from playing out worst-case scenarios as he kept his eyes forward. If the ice broke beneath them, he would end up a squashed bug on one of the rocks.

The bridge took a steep descent and Jack fell and slid the rest of the way. He raised his hands over his face and prepared for impact, but it never came. Instead, he slowed to a halt right outside the mouth of a dark cavern. Aria stood over him, her hands on her hips in a superhero pose, and looked at him with amusement.

"Having fun?"

Jack's cheeks burned as he got to his feet and marched forward, ignoring the question.

As they entered deeper into the cavern, the noise outside became dull, but the pirate's screams still echoed in Jack's ears.

"So, you don't think we should go back and help them?"

Aria glanced at him with a puzzled look. "*Them* who? I don't save pirates. Especially not in mermaid-infested waters. Besides, if they're busy out there, that means no one is in here."

Jack didn't argue, but something twinged inside at the sound of mermaid-*infested* waters. He couldn't help but notice the disdain in her voice.

Aria took a torch from its holder and carried it as they drew deeper into the cave. It was as big as the ogre's cave, but much to Jack's relief, this one did not smell like rotten eggs.

"Here." Aria roughly passed the torch to Jack, narrowly missing his face. The flames licked his hair before he pulled it away from his body. Undeterred, Aria ran across the open cave, her shoes splashing the puddles and footsteps echoing.

"How good are you at swimming?" she asked, shooting him a look as she removed her cloak.

Jack swallowed nervously. "I'm practically a fish."

Aria kicked off her shoes and rolled her hair into a bun. "Good. Because we need to swim into the next cave." She pointed at a mouth of water sitting innocently in the corner.

"How do you know it's not here?" Jack asked, gesturing to the stacks of wooden crates and chests. Aria frowned at him.

"Come on. They're not going to hide their treasure in here. Anyone could come along and take it." She rolled up her sleeves as Jack set down the torch and removed his own cloak.

"How do you know where we're going? Have you been here before?"

Aria didn't answer but her face said it all.

"Wow, you really are the greatest thief in the forest." For a second, Jack caught a glimmer of pride wash over her face, but it quickly settled into a focused stare as she disappeared beneath the water.

Jack looked around to check he was still alone,

then crouched and took a deep breath. He expected the water to be bitter cold, and the logical part of his brain insisted that it was. But when he immersed himself, it was like bathing in a bath of warm honey. He had lied to Aria. He was not that fond of water, or swimming into the unknown. But the thought of being left behind gave him worse chills.

He pushed through, following the ethereal light coming from ahead. Not too much longer now. His lungs protested. He was never very good at holding his breath.

The manor had a swimming pool where Jack spent many nights close to tears. His grandfather insisted on pushing Jack to swim faster. Hold his breath longer. All while Jack hated being in the water.

Bitter memories came rushing back as Jack slowed his pace. The water grew heavy, pushing him down as his heartbeat flooded his ears.

"Don't stop now. You're almost there."

The sound of his grandfather's voice startled him. And the water around him began to freeze. His body twitched as his muscles screamed in agony. Air. He needed air. Aria's face appeared in his mind and with renewed strength he pressed on, reaching out and fanning his hands back like a frog. His ears were ringing, and for a split second he thought that this was it. He wasn't going to be killed by ogres, mermaids, or a revengeful story-book character. No. He would drown trying to catch up to Aria. But just as the thought crossed his mind, the light flooded the water above him and he pushed upwards. Then his head broke the surface, and he took the most glorious breath of fresh air. A pair of hands grabbed him under the arms and he stumbled out onto the rocky floor.

"I was wondering what was taking you so long." Aria stooped down and looked at him with worry. Strands of damp hair stuck to her temples, but she didn't seem to notice.

"You know, I can't help but think you're going to be the death of me," Jack said, getting to his feet, still taking greedy gulps of oxygen.

Aria smirked and gave him a shove.

"Well, while you were taking your sweet time paddling, I've been looking through all this—"

Jack gasped. Around them sat piles of... junk? He was expecting to see more gold and precious jewels. Not a bunch of forks and coins of little value.

"Are you sure this is a pirate cave?" he asked,

shaking water out of his hair. Aria walked away and kneeled down beside a chest. At least there was a chest.

"Who cares. We don't have long. Help me look."

The two of them searched through the treasure chest in silence. The coins were huge. Some of them as big as Jack's palm. And glass bottles stuffed with scrolls were stacked up in the corners. He itched to open one and read them. How many stories were there to unfold? What secrets might they discover?

But their search was in vain.

"I don't understand. It was definitely here." Aria scratched her head and frowned. Jack joined her.

"You don't know of any more pirate caves, do you?" he asked. Aria looked at him unimpressed. "Okay, then it has to be here. Maybe we're missing something."

Suddenly, a heavenly song broke their conversation. Jack craned his neck. "Do you hear that?"

All of the pain in his body fizzled away, and he staggered toward the voice like a drunken sailor, his whole resolve melted.

"Oh great. Just what we need." Aria huffed.

She grabbed Jack's arm and shook him, but the irritation in her voice had Jack confused. How could the enchanting sound annoy her? How was Aria not in a bubble of eternal bliss?

"It's… beautiful," he whispered, his face breaking into a goofy grin.

More voices joined the song in a transcendental symphony of melodies. As he drew closer to the sounds, Jack could just make out the words.

Still and quiet, always. Fill our hearts with wonder. Never knowing pain or sorrow.

Aria smacked Jack's face, and he snapped out of the trance.

"Don't listen to it," she said, waving a finger at him. "Let's keep looking."

He could still hear it, but it was faint. He walked toward the water's edge. Something shined underneath. *Could it be the shard?* he thought, focusing his eyes on the iridescent reflection coming from under the water.

"Jack, get back!"

Before Jack could react to Aria's words, a mermaid grabbed him by his shirt and pulled him in. He held his breath as the water washed over him. Her arms locked him in a strong grip. He kicked, searching for the ground, but there was nothing. He was going to drown.

Suddenly, he was thrust back to the surface and took a deep, gasping breath. He blinked furiously, wiping water from his face and looking around the cave. A silver hand mirror was propped up on a pile of junk, and he could see the reflection of a mermaid holding him from behind. He inwardly gasped.

"Let him go," Aria barked, creating a ball of ice in her hand.

"I wouldn't do that if I were you." The unnaturally perfect-looking young woman bobbed in the water behind him. Her dark hair covered her slender shoulders, and while holding him like a hostage, she looked at Jack through the mirror with deep, penetrating eyes. Her rosy lips curved upwards and his stomach flipped. "You don't want him to end up like your betrothed, do you?"

Betrothed?

"Don't look at her, Jack!" Aria's voice jolted him and their eye contact broke. The ice in Aria's hand melted, and she reached for her knife.

"How did you find my cave?" the mermaid asked. Her voice, though firm, was still too delicate for a monster. "What are you looking for?"

Jack kept his eyes on Aria, but when a fork rose to his face, he let out a chuckle.

"What's so funny?" the mermaid asked, her voice just behind his ear.

"Nothing," Jack replied. "I just thought that was a hairbrush for you." When neither girl laughed, he realized they wouldn't understand the reference and he cleared his throat. "Okay, how about we all lower the weapons, huh?"

When the alluring song started again, Jack clamped his hands over his ears. The mermaid tightened her grip around his chest to the point that he could barely breathe.

"Let him go!" Aria demanded, clutching the knife so tightly her knuckles were turning white.

When the song came to an abrupt end, Jack looked at her reflection in the mirror again. She was shaking her head as if coming out of a trance.

"Not until you tell me what you took from my cave."

"Nothing," Jack wheezed, dropping his hands. "We didn't take anything."

"Then what are you doing here?"

"Aria…" Jack motioned for her to put her knife down. "Trust me."

She put her knife away begrudgingly, and the mermaid loosened her grip. Jack gasped for air. "Thank you."

"Start talking." And just like that, the fork was back at his face as if it were a weapon. Though, if she aimed it at his eyes, she could blind him. Then he'd be like the ogre. He shook the thought away.

"Okay, so…" Jack said. "We're looking for a—"

"Jack, don't tell her anything." Aria glared at the mermaid.

"It's okay," Jack said to Aria. "She can help us."

"How could a mermaid possibly be helpful?" Aria hissed.

"If the shard were here, she would know where it is," Jack reasoned. "Besides, if she wanted to kill me, she would've done it already." Jack looked at the mermaid's reflection in the mirror as she held him from behind. "Isn't that right?"

The mermaid didn't respond, but she did let him go. Jack swam and grabbed onto the rocks. Aria hurried to his aid, pulling him out of the water. By the time he turned back to the mermaid, she was sitting on the rocks, looking at them with narrow eyes.

"So, you're looking for the shard?" she asked, and Aria's eyes widened.

"You know about the shard?"

The mermaid nodded. "But it's not here."

"Then where is it?" Aria asked. Even though Jack was not looking at her, he could pick up the desperation in her voice. If the shard was lost, all hope of her escape would be too.

"I can tell you…" The mermaid said so simply and sweetly, it was hard for Jack to believe this creature could harm anyone. "But first I want to know, where did you get that necklace?"

"How about you answer my question first," Aria shot back.

A sickly sweet giggle followed, then a splash. Jack was scanning the surface when the mermaid shot out of the water and landed beside them on the rocky ground. Instead of legs, she had a magnificent tail with sparkling scales and a fin that shimmered in the sunshine breaking through the rocks. Beads of water clung to her skin and her hair sat at her waist, no sign of a single tangle.

"Who are you?" Jack asked, still mesmerized by the mermaid's beauty.

"I'm Lexa. Daughter of Poseidon and protector of innocent life."

Jack frowned at her as he stood. "You killed those men."

Aria elbowed him in the ribs without looking back. "Where is the shard?" she pressed.

Lexa studied her fingernails with her brows arched as she simpered. "Those were not men." She looked at Jack, who took a step back. The heat of her gaze unnerved him. "They stole from my sisters. And killed our friends. Do you think it's wrong for us to wipe their wretched species from this place?"

Jack found himself shaking his head despite himself. Aria stomped on his foot.

"Stop it. We can't trust her."

"My father has the mirror shard," Lexa said finally. "It was taken to him shortly before you arrived."

"Can we get it back?" Jack asked.

Lexa looked at him with a mixture of sympathy and amusement. "*You* can't. It's where I live. At the bottom of the sea."

Jack's heart sank, and he exchanged a look with Aria, whose face had turned pale.

"But *I* can get it for you," Lexa added.

"And why would you do that for us?" Aria asked.

Lexa looked into the water wistfully and played with her hair. Tiny flecks of snow fell through the cracks above them and settled on the water's surface, making it look like something out of a snow globe.

"If you let me have your necklace, I will get you the shard."

Aria grasped her necklace like it possessed her soul. "It was my mother's. It's all I have left of her."

Lexa drummed her fingers against her arm. "That's my deal. The shard for the necklace."

"Why is it so important to you?" Aria asked, her voice shaken. But Jack couldn't fathom why. It was just a necklace, and Lexa's deal was more than fair. But this was the Chanted Forest, not Oxford. And nothing was what it seemed, so he decided to stay out of it.

"That doesn't concern you. Now, make your decision," Lexa said, crossing her arms. Her dark eyes fluttered at Jack and she beamed at him. "Or you can let me have *him*."

Aria tugged on the necklace and held it out. "Fine. You can have it," she said quickly. Lexa grinned as she reached for it, but Aria pulled it away. "As soon as you bring me the shard."

Lexa frowned then shot Jack a scowl. His brain turned to mush, and before he realized what he was doing, he snatched the necklace from Aria's hand.

"Jack, no!"

He threw it to Lexa, and she caught it with a smile, studying it in her hands. Her fingers grazed the rock pendant and she smiled at it as if looking at an old friend.

Aria grabbed her wrist and pointed the knife to her face. "You better bring me that mirror."

Lexa nodded and disappeared into the water.

"What just happened?" Jack asked, puzzled.

"*Mermaids* happened," Aria hissed. "It's what they do."

When Aria said nothing else, Jack turned to face her with a nagging thought. "You were engaged?" he asked as she rubbed the back of her neck and sat on the rocky floor. "It was George, wasn't it? I thought you said he didn't mean anything."

"It was an arranged marriage," she explained. "It was the only way to bring peace to our kingdom."

"At seventeen? That's a lot of pressure."

Aria sighed as she hugged her knees. "Enough about me. Tell me more about *your* land."

Jack shrugged, taking a seat next to her. "It's different, I guess. Not that I've seen very much. Grandfather kept me in the manor for most of my life. And he was not a fan of technology. I didn't even own a smartphone until I was fourteen."

Aria looked at him with her brows furrowed. "A what?"

"It's a device where you can communicate with people or find out anything you want to know."

Jack had barely thought about his home since he fell through the mirror. It was funny how little he missed his phone and gadgets.

"You always talk about your grandfather... what happened to your parents?"

The question nipped at Jack's heart. His parents were a sore topic. "I was very young when they died. I hardly remember them."

"I'm sorry," Aria said, looking away. She didn't have to say it, he knew she'd also lost her parents. Jack's stomach knotted as a blanket of sadness washed over them. He had an urge to wrap his arms around Aria again. As if the action would somehow soothe his own troubled soul. But just as the thought crossed his mind, an unearthly scream shot into the air like a cannon.

Jack's blood drained from his face. "Lexa."

Aria scrambled to her feet, her knife out already and expression fierce. "The shard!" She dashed across the rocky floor, jumping over a puddle and disappeared in a small opening in the cave wall.

Jack edged sideways through a narrow passage and joined Aria back on the sandy beach. "Why couldn't we have gone in this way?" he asked, looking around the deserted shores.

The alluring song started again, but this time the song was filled with sorrow, like orcas crying. Aria shot him another look, but then their eyes locked on the massive ship that had been innocently bobbing in the distance.

"There she is!" Jack pointed at the glittering fin splashing in the distance. A large net appeared from beneath the water and a mermaid thrashed about beneath a crane.

Jack and Aria exchanged a look as deep roars of delight and celebration filled the air amidst the mermaid's screams.

Aria darted toward the ocean without a word,

but Jack grabbed her arm. "Wait, we can't just go at them without a plan."

"The plan is to get the shard from her before they do!" Aria ran toward the shore, then stretched out her hands, creating yet another ice bridge on the water. When she skated on top of it, Jack followed.

But the ice stopped forming out of her hands, and the ice bridge began to thin. Jack slipped and stumbled forward, crashing onto Aria's back. They fell and spun on the thin ice until they lost momentum.

"Sorry," Jack said, pushing himself to his knees. A crack split the ice in front of him and he looked at Aria.

"Jack…" she breathed as she watched the crack slowly grow between Jack's legs. He looked up at her again, blood draining from his face.

"Don't move," she mouthed, and he gulped, barely breathing.

She stretched her hand toward the crack to try to mend it, but nothing happened. She looked at her hand as if something was wrong then tried again. Her brows furrowed.

"What's wrong?" Jack asked.

"I don't know," she said, turning toward the

ship in the distance and waving her hands with a frown. "My powers are gone."

"What?" Jack grabbed her hand to take a closer look. Her palms were frozen, so her powers were still there. But before he could register another thought, the same beautiful melody overtook his thoughts again, and Jack lifted his head toward the blissful sound. "Do you hear that?"

"Jack, don't!"

As soon as he turned his body, the ice cracked under their weight and they crashed into the water with a loud splash. The impact jolted him out of the trance.

"Jack, swim!" Aria screamed behind him, and when he turned around to find her, all he saw were the iridescent fins charging after them. "Hurry!"

A wave of adrenaline shocked him like a defibrillator and he started flailing his arms against the icy water. A whistle echoed behind them, perhaps a mermaid call, and it pushed him to swim faster.

As soon as their feet hit the sand again, he stood and ran next to Aria toward the grassy patch near a tree. He dropped to his knees, out of breath. A handful of mermaids lifted their heads from the water to give them one last glare before disappearing back into the ocean.

Jack let out a breath of relief while Aria collapsed next to him.

"What do we do now?" he asked her, exasperated.

Aria grunted as she narrowed her eyes at the ship already shrinking in the distance. "Looks like we're going fishing."

ARIA

*A*ria pinned Ryke against the wall of the tavern, holding her knife to his throat. Jack touched her shoulder, but she didn't loosen her grip.

"And what makes you think I'll help you after you double crossed me?" Ryke asked. There was no fear in his eyes when he met Aria's scowl.

"Just answer the question," she hissed, pressing the blade to his scruffy skin. "Who are those pirates, and where would they take a mermaid?"

Ryke arched a brow. "Since when do you care what happens to a mermaid?" By the disdain in his tone, he didn't like them either. At least they had that in common.

"I don't," Aria snapped. "She took something of mine, and I want it back."

"And what's in it for me?" Ryke flashed a smug smile, and Aria growled.

"How about you get to live?" She pressed the blade to his neck again.

"All right, enough." Jack pulled Aria off of Ryke and watched as he rubbed his neck. "Tell us what you know."

Ryke looked from Aria to Jack. "Fine, but I'll need something in return."

"Please, let me cut his tongue out," Aria muttered to Jack, but he raised a hand.

"What do you want?"

Ryke turned to Jack, and Aria felt an uneasiness in the pit of her stomach.

"After we save your precious mermaid, you come with me."

"Absolutely not," Aria barked. And how many times did she have to say she couldn't care less about saving the mermaid?

"Where will you take me?" Jack asked.

"Not where, mate." Ryke smoothed his shirt. "To *whom*."

Aria didn't like the curiosity in Jack's eyes. "You can't trust him," she whispered.

"He knew I was coming through the portal," Jack reminded her. "So, whoever this person is, they may know why I'm here."

Aria opened her mouth to protest, but there was nothing she could say to change his mind. Especially when he was determined to get answers. And to be fair, he deserved them. He'd done so much to help her.

"Fine…" she grumbled, and Jack's face lit up.

He turned to Ryke with renewed enthusiasm. "Seems like you got yourself a deal… mate." Jack offered his hand, but Ryke didn't bother taking it.

"You don't get to say *mate*, mate."

Jack's smile fell, and Aria wanted to slap Ryke for being a jerk. "So, where do we go from here?" Aria asked, putting her knife away.

"Where do you think?" Ryke cocked his head smugly. "The Dark Howler."

*T*he pirate ship's deck swarmed with Ryke's men, swinging from the rigging as the wind slapped and ballooned the giant sails. But Aria wasn't paying attention to any of it. She kept her focus on her hands as it reflected the bright light of the moon. A wisp of ice covered her palms but then quickly vanished. She grunted in frustration, then slapped her hands on the back railing.

"Still not working?" Jack asked, coming to stand next to her and holding a piece of cooked fish. "Here, you should eat something." He handed her a piece, which she gladly took.

"It doesn't help that I'm exhausted," she said, already chewing. "My powers are still in me, but I'm so drained, I can't seem to tap into them."

"What do you think it is?" Jack asked, leaning back against the wooden rail to face her.

"My mother's necklace," she replied, looking out over the expanse of the sea. "It amplified my powers. Without it, I have to rely entirely on my own strength."

"What was so special about it?"

"It's a mermaid stone," she said.

"But you said your powers are still in you, right?" Jack asked, and Aria nodded. "Then maybe your body just needs time to adjust." He touched Aria's shoulder, encouragingly. "I'm sure you'll be fine."

She nodded as the wind blew, sending an icy chill between them.

"There they are!" Ryke called out from across the ship, looking through a spyglass.

The massive galleon bobbed under a dark storm cloud. A bolt of lightning struck in the distance, lighting up the unmistakable skull and crossbones flag of another pirate ship.

Aria's heart nearly burst through her chest when an ear-splitting boom lit up the sea a few feet away. She crouched, pulling Jack down with her, and covered her head. A cannonball careened into the water mere feet from where they stood.

The ship's floorboards groaned, followed by a raucous thud and a shout. "Fire!" A roaring boom shook the galleon. Hurried footsteps clamored around them as Ryke bellowed commands, his voice high pitched and quick. She didn't trust the man, not one bit, but his confidence was enough to fill her with a strange sense of ease. He commanded that ship like he owned the world.

Another boom erupted from the cannon, lighting up the night sky as it crashed onto the enemy's galleon. Aria jumped to her feet then stepped up on the rail and stretched out her hands toward the dark waters. Ice structures shot from her hands and began to form an ice plank across the space between the ships. But then it stopped and the plank hung unfinished.

Another cannon blasted from the enemy's ship, shattering the only piece of ice she was able to form. She grunted in frustration. *I guess I'll have to do this the regular way.*

She removed her cloak—which she had retrieved from the cavern—and let it drop behind her.

"Aria, wait!" Jack called out, but she didn't want to waste any more time. She dove into the water, which muffled the sound of the explosions above, as well as Jack's voice as he called out to her. She held her breath and swam toward the pirate's ship as quickly as she could manage. By the time she surfaced out of the water, she had reached the enemy's ship. Grabbing on to the rope, she looked back to find Jack watching her, wide-eyed.

She smiled. *He looked cute when he worried.*

More blasts rocked the ship as Aria climbed to the deck. As soon as she jumped onboard, Lexa's melodic voice came from across the boat. She hung, tangled in a net above a tall man with dirty blonde hair who looked like the ship's captain.

"Fire!" he yelled again, and Aria hid behind a

wooden barrel. The floorboards shook under her weight, and when she peeked out, her eyes locked with Lexa's who was hanging on a net over the captain's head. She was holding a bag in her hands, and Aria knew the shard was in there. But what she needed the most was the necklace. Aria wouldn't be able to fight those men without her powers. Even if she did get her hands on a sword.

The winds suddenly picked up with greater force, and the men on the galleon had to anchor themselves down so as not to be blown away. Aria grabbed the rope she'd used to climb and pushed against the icy gust of wind that rushed over the ship.

"Why aren't we firing?" the captain yelled.

"The cannons are frozen, sir!" one of the men replied with a panicked voice. "And their ship is getting closer!"

"Then grab your weapons!"

Hurried footsteps ran toward the rail, and once they crouched in position, they clicked their guns.

"Fire!" the captain ordered, and the blast of gunshots filled the air.

Aria pulled out her knife and held it between her teeth as she jumped on one of the sails. Once she reached the rope she was looking for, she started cutting.

"Hey!" A man's voice came from behind her and she whipped around. He charged toward her, but she kicked him in the face. When his back slammed against the floor, she shifted her attention back to cutting the rope above her head. By the time the rest of the men turned in her direction, the rope snapped, driving a large wooden beam toward them. Most jumped out of the way, but some fell overboard. Their screams filled the air, but only until they hit the water.

"Get the girl!" the captain ordered.

Aria used the cut rope to swing over the men's heads toward Lexa's net. Lexa stuck her hand out from the net and Aria grabbed on to her.

A gunshot blasted in the air, and Aria ducked. Before they could recharge their weapons, she climbed over Lexa's net and hid from sight.

"Hold your fire!" the captain yelled, drawing his sword and pointing toward the net. "Don't hurt the mermaid!"

"Give me the necklace back," Aria demanded, pushing her hand through the net.

"I don't have it. I hid it before coming back to the surface," Lexa replied. "But I can buy you some time!" She dug into her bag and pulled out just enough of the shard to catch the reflection of the moonlight. Grabbing her bag with both hands, she angled it so it reflected toward the men looking up at them. As soon as the moonlight's reflection from the shard hit their eyes, they began to fight one another as if they were bitter enemies.

"How did you know to do that?" Aria asked, looking down at the brawling men.

"How do you ask for a shard when you know nothing about it?" Lexa retorted with an attitude, and Aria gladly cut the last bit of rope that held the net, letting Lexa fall on the main deck with a hard thud. She jumped down, landing next to Lexa who was still tangled on the net.

"Step away from the mermaid!" the captain demanded, his sword still drawn.

Aria turned around with her knife in hand, but he hit her blade with his sword, sending it flying overboard. Before she could make another move, the captain pressed the tip of his sword to her neck.

"Blink and you die," he hissed.

"Let the lass go, mate." Ryke's voice boomed from across the ship, his sword drawn as well.

"Aria!" Jack appeared beside him, the blood drained from his face.

The captain grabbed Aria and turned her around, pinning her back to his chest. "Then get off my ship," he growled, bringing his sword to Aria's throat.

"You're not a pirate," Ryke said, jumping down to the main deck. He pointed to the skull and crossbones on the flag waving above their heads. "You expect to fool anyone with that?" The captain stepped back, taking Aria with him. "You work for the King of the Shores, don't you?"

The captain didn't deny it.

"What does the king want with a mermaid?" Ryke asked, twirling his sword.

"That does not concern you," he replied through clenched teeth. "None of you. Now, step back or she dies." He pressed the blade hard to her skin, and Aria winced.

"As you wish, mate." Ryke leapt toward Lexa and put his sword to her neck. "You kill her... and I'll slice your precious mermaid."

The captain's jaw tightened, and by the way his hands were shaking, Aria knew he was torn. For some reason, he needed the mermaid alive, and Ryke knew just how to play his cards.

"Fine." The captain lifted his hands and stepped away from Aria. "Take her and go. Just leave me the fish."

Aria ran across the deck to her bag, grabbing it and strapping it on. Lexa, who was still tangled in the net, grabbed Aria's foot. Her pleading eyes glistening with the reflection of her iridescent fin.

"Please, don't leave me."

Aria met her eyes but only for a moment. "Our deal is done." She yanked her foot from Lexa's grip and ran back toward Jack.

"Take my ship and go. My men will take you back," Ryke said to Aria, all while keeping his eyes —as well as his sword—pointed toward the captain. "Looks like I have unfinished business here."

"Thanks, Ryke." Aria turned to Jack. "Let's get out of here."

"Wait, what?" Jack grabbed her arm before she took another step. "We can't leave Lexa."

"We didn't come here for her," Aria said, keeping her voice low. "We came for the shard. Now, let's go." She pulled Jack by his arm, but he yanked it free and stepped away from her.

"No," he said firmly. "I won't leave her."

"Is she singing in your head again?" Aria grumbled, turning to glare at Lexa.

"She's not," Jack assured her. "But we can't just leave her to die after she helped us."

"It wasn't a *favor*, Jack," Aria reminded him. "It was a trade. She got the necklace, and we got the shard."

"You can't possibly be that coldhearted."

His words stung more than she thought they would. She'd been called many things before, especially by the people she stole from during her days with Robin, but never had anyone's opinion of her ever mattered. Not until now.

She turned to watch as Ryke and the captain continued exchanging words about the King of the Shores and whatnot. She didn't care about any of it. She just wanted to get the stupid shard and disappear from that world forever.

"Oh, flipping heck." Aria lunged at one of the sailors and took his sword. "Go free her!" she yelled to Jack as her sword clanged with another. And another.

The sailors kept charging at her, but she fought them swiftly and elegantly, all while keeping an eye on Jack as he tried to cut Lexa loose.

Ryke was engaged in his own private fight with the captain, but he was getting dangerously close to Jack, despite Ryke's attempt to keep him at bay.

"Hurry, Jack!" Aria yelled, stealing for herself a second sword as three sailors came at her, screaming as if that would somehow give them an advantage. They each received a lightning-quick kick to their stomachs, turning their screams to whimpers.

Jack dragged Lexa toward the plank, then helped her over the rail. She gave him a grateful nod then jumped into the water, still tangled in the net.

"No!" The captain kicked Ryke in the stomach then lunged toward Jack with his sword in a rage.

Aria ran and pushed Jack out of the way, her shoulder taking the full force of the captain's blade. Her breathing cut short as her back hit the railing. The captain watched in shock as particles of ice covered his entire sword.

He pulled back. "You're the princess," he murmured, his eyes wide as he stared at the frozen sword. But then his lips curved up and he yanked the sword from her shoulder.

Aria grimaced.

"We've hit the jackpot, boys." He grabbed Aria in a firm grip then turned around to his sailors. "Throw them overboard."

The men who had been watching the commotion grabbed their weapons with renewed determination and charged at Jack. Ryke threw him one of his swords as he jumped to his feet, and Jack caught it mid-air.

Aria tried fighting the captain off as he dragged her toward the lower deck, but the pain in her shoulder was so excruciating, it made her head spin. Her eyes locked with Jack's as he helped Ryke fight off the sailors.

"Jack—" Her voice was cut off as the captain pinned her to the wall. "Why are you doing this?" she breathed, biting back the pain.

"The Queen has a very generous bounty on your head." He flashed her a steely smile. "Turns out, you're worth more than a thousand mermaids."

He dragged her down the steps then pushed her into a small room. She fell to the floor, hitting her injured shoulder on the small bed in the corner, and cried out in pain. She pushed herself up, biting back a grimace as she yanked on the door. It was locked.

The boat rocked, throwing her off balance, and she dropped to the floor again. She stretched out her hand toward the door, but there was nothing. Not even a wisp of ice.

"Jack..." She crawled toward the door and banged on it with the little strength she had left. But then she closed her eyes and whispered, almost like a prayer, "I need you."

JACK

Jack's body buzzed with adrenaline. Swords clashed, men grunted, and the ship rocked to the side so suddenly, it threw several sailors off their feet. Screams of agony flooded the air, but it was all just noise. Nothing could distract Jack from the blaze of energy bubbling under his skin. He kicked his attacker then turned to the next one. Meanwhile, Ryke dealt with the men on the other side of him.

"Where's Aria?" Jack shouted over his shoulder to Ryke. An overly eager sailor slammed his blade against Jack's and groaned as he leaned in. He was barely older than a boy. His mop of blonde hair was damp with sweat and his eyes were full of fear. Jack grit his teeth and pushed him back, then swiped his legs and the boy fell with a thud.

He glanced back at Ryke just as he beat a sailor with the handle of his sword.

"They took her below deck," Ryke grunted. "Go. My men will handle these fools."

Jack didn't need to be told twice. He charged across the deck, hopping over wounded sailors, and balled his hands into fists. The sky grew darker and the supernatural winds howled around the ship like a cyclone. He halted and ducked as a sailor flew past him, picked up by the wind. The ferocious sea tossed the ship, sending it flying into Ryke's vessel with a crash. Screams and shouts were muffled by the crunch of the collision, and Jack jumped back just as a piece of timber fell to his feet.

"The ships are sinking!" someone yelled.

The sailors and pirates stopped fighting and turned their attention to their own ships.

"Quick. Get back aboard," Ryke yelled.

Jack watched Ryke gather the rest of his crew, and they scrambled over the edge and disappeared while the remaining sailors ran around like headless chickens. The captain reappeared from below deck, his face free of color as his beady eyes took in the disastrous sight. Jack's chest burned and every muscle in his body tensed as he charged for the captain, ready to impale him with every inch of his sword.

But the howling wind knocked the captain back. He dropped his sword and the back of his head struck the mast, sending him to his knees. He fell on his face and lay motionless on the sodden deck.

Water lapped at Jack's feet as the boat leaned on its side and descended into the sea.

Aria.

Jack's heart raced as he dropped the sword and scrambled over the bodies, then ran below deck. Once his feet touched the floor, the water reached his thighs. He covered his mouth and nose with a hand to stifle the dank scent, then dragged his legs forward as he trudged through the rising water, looking for Aria.

At the end of the narrow hall was a door with a window. The elaborately carved iron lock told Jack it must have been the captain's quarters. By the time he reached it, the water was at his waist.

He slammed his fist against the window. "Aria!"

A moment later, Aria's pale face appeared and her eyes grew glassy as she shouted back to him. But her voice was too muffled through the thick door.

"Hold on, I'm going to get you out of there!" Jack shouted as loud as he could. He grabbed the handle and shoved, but the door didn't move. He dragged a hand through his hair in frustration.

Why didn't I bring the sword with me?

He considered going back for it, but the water was rising so fast, he knew there wasn't time. Instead, he looked around him. A small lantern hung on the wall, he took it off the hook and shouted again.

"Stand back!" With a smash, he hit the glass with the lantern and beat the glass fragments away. "Are you okay?"

The window was just big enough for Jack to reach through. He waved around until his arms collided with something solid. A hand grabbed his and gave it a squeeze.

"Jack. You need to go," Aria said in a firm voice. She thrust a bag in Jack's hand. "Take the shard. Use the mirror and get away from this place."

"I'm not leaving you," Jack said as the water crept up to his chest. He pushed the bag back in Aria's hand and cradled her face, grazing her cheek with his thumb.

"There's no way out, Jack. I'm done for." Aria's voice broke and Jack stooped down to see her wide eyes through the window.

"No one is dying today." He held his breath, withdrew his hand and crouched under the water, bracing as he leaned back. Then he plowed all of his weight into the door. But the force merely sent a dull pain through his shoulder. He tried again. And again. But it was no use, and he was growing dizzy as his lungs screamed for air. He floated and gasped as his face broke the surface of the water.

"Aria, hold on," he gurgled as the water hovered barely an inch from the ceiling. He took a deep breath and dove down, reaching through the window. He grasped her hand and caught sight of Aria's face. She looked at him imploringly, mouthing the word 'go,' but Jack shook his head and squeezed.

He couldn't leave her.

Just when he had resigned to their twisted fate,

a movement from behind caught his attention. A flash of sparkly light flooded his vision and he wondered if this was the heavenly light people talked about. But then a face came into view and Jack gasped, choking on the water. He let go of Aria's hand and lurched back as his body jerked, begging to break free of his watery cell. Then the most transcendent sound filled his ears, the same unearthly song he had heard back at the cavern. Only in the water it sounded a thousand times more enchanting. Jack's body grew limp and he relaxed, all pain and struggle gone.

The door wrenched open, and Jack smiled serenely as he watched the mermaid reach in and retrieve Aria, who floated unconscious.

The mermaid turned toward him, her dark hair waving in the water in a whimsical fashion.

Lexa.

Suddenly, filled with an unknown energy, he dragged his arms and legs through the water. Once he used the base of the stairwell to propel himself upwards, he looked back to find Lexa behind him, carrying Aria in her arms. Happy that Aria was in good hands, he turned back and climbed the ladder.

The music gave him renewed strength as if his

body was somehow able to function so long as the singing continued.

A bright light flooded the surface and grew stronger as he drew closer. With a final glance behind him, he kicked his feet and his head crashed through the water and he gave in to the biggest gasp of his entire life.

The two ships had fully submerged into the water with only debris floating around them. The dark clouds were gone as the sunrise peeked over the horizon, bathing the sea in a soft pink glow.

A large wooden door floated to his left. He reached for it as Aria's head appeared, along with the mermaid.

"Lexa. You came back for us," Jack said, thankful.

Lexa inclined her head. "You saved me, so I saved you. Now, my debt has been repaid."

"Where are the rest of the mermaids?" Jack asked.

"We're not allowed to attack in Elven territory," Lexa explained, helping Jack lift Aria onto the door. She coughed and spluttered, much to Jack's relief. But the dark bloodstain on her shirt had his stomach churning.

"Her shoulder is still bleeding. We need to get

her to land," he said as he climbed onto the door and settled next to Aria. She moaned and moved her head, but kept her eyes shut.

"Hold on to something," Lexa said, her voice firm. Jack held Aria with one hand and clamped his other hand around the edge of the door as Lexa positioned herself behind them. Then, they moved forward at a break-neck speed. Sprays of water washed over them as the door sped across the water like a surfboard. The door bumped against the rippling current, and soon Jack could make out the outline of an island in the distance.

"What is that?" he shouted over the rushing sound of them racing through the sea. Despite the speed they were going, Lexa's reply was not breathless as he expected, but calm and even. It was as if she were merely taking a pleasant stroll in the park and not zooming across the ocean.

"The closest island… there are people who dwell on it who will be able to help Aria."

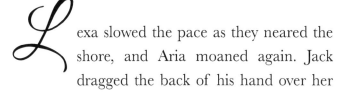

exa slowed the pace as they neared the shore, and Aria moaned again. Jack dragged the back of his hand over her clammy forehead and frowned. She was burning up.

"This is where I leave you. I have to go back," Lexa said, gently pushing the door onto the sand. "And please, give this to Aria." She handed Aria's knife to Jack. "I used it to free myself from the net. Thank you for saving my life, Jack. I hope you find what you're looking for."

"Wait," Jack turned to Lexa. "About the necklace. Will Aria lose her powers without it?"

"No," Lexa replied. "The stone simply recharged her powers. She'll just need to pace herself and save her energy." And with that, Lexa backed away.

"Thank you," Jack said with a nod. A small smile crossed her face and then she disappeared with a splash.

Jack scooped up Aria in his arms and staggered along the beach, looking for any sign of life. Tall trees towered over them, their lush green leaves providing shelter from the sunshine. But the sea air had a bite to it, Aria shivered in his arms and mumbled something incoherent.

"It's all right, I'm getting you some help," Jack said soothingly. Aria buried her face in his chest and his heart squeezed. Her body grew limp when she lost consciousness again as Jack stumbled away from the sea and deeper into the woods.

"Can somebody help me, please?" Jack set his jaw and ignored his aching muscles as they protested with every step. Sticks snapped beneath his feet and he left a trail of water leading all the way back to the shore.

A squirrel scarpered up a tree trunk and looked at him with curiosity. Somewhere in the distance a bird called. Jack followed a path that had light footprints. They were shallow but recent.

"Please, my friend is hurt. I need someone to help her."

A snap of a twig to Jack's left had him halt and on high alert. With Aria's unconscious body in his arms and no weapon to hand, he was vulnerable. "Who's there?"

A bush rustled and a fluffy white rabbit hopped out and scampered away. Jack sighed and turned, then he almost dropped Aria with a gasp.

Three tall women wearing white cloaks and with hair as golden as the setting sun stood in his path. Their eyes focused on Jack with such intensity, he couldn't help get the feeling that they knew who he was. But that was impossible.

"Excuse me, I'm sorry to intrude on your land. But my friend is awfully wounded and requires assistance." Jack tried to sound polite and gentlemanly. But his voice shook. One of the women raised her hands and lowered the hood of her cloak. The tips of her pointy ears peeked through her hair and her face radiated light as she smiled at him.

Pointy ears. Are they elves?

"All is well, Jack. We have been expecting you." Her voice was light as a feather, but the words rang in his ears. "Is Ryke with you?"

Ryke? Is this where he wanted to take Jack?

"No, he's not. And how do you know me?" he stuttered. Two of the women walked forward and reached out for Aria, but Jack stepped back. "Who are you people?"

"Come, let us take your friend." The woman's voice was heavenly. "The Healer can help."

"The Healer? I'm not leaving Aria." Jack stepped back, holding Aria closer to his chest as he stared at the elegant women walking closer.

One of them laughed softly. "Then let us take you to him."

Jack followed them deeper into the woods. His

mind raced with questions, but he got the impression that these elves would talk in riddles.

Birds sang from the treetops, and glimmers of sunshine peeped through the leaves like spotlights. The air on this island seemed to breathe. As if the land was also a living thing. With every inhale, Jack was flooded with a sense of peace and tranquility. The sensation of "all is well" impressed itself on his mind.

They reached a wooden hut nestled in the trees, and Jack stopped.

"He is waiting." One of the women gestured for Jack to enter, but he hesitated. Walking into the unknown had him on edge. What if he was being lured into a trap?

Aria stirred in his arms and he cradled her close. Her face was pale and soaked in sweat and her lips were turning blue. There was no other choice. Aria needed the Healer—whoever he was. So despite the fact he may well be an enemy, Jack knew he had to save Aria, whatever the cost. He took a deep breath, inhaling the calming air and allowed it to flood his senses. Then he walked inside.

The hut was much larger on the inside than it looked from outside. A wooden table sat in the center of the room, and stacks of shelves with glass bottles and leather-bound books lined the walls. Parchment papers littered the desk. All manner of interesting trinkets filled the hut. But none of it mattered. Jack just stared at the man cloaked in white, standing beside a bed. His face was engraved with fine wrinkles, and his wiry blonde hair had a little gray to it. But Jack could never mistake those clear, penetrating eyes.

"Grandfather?" he whispered.

"Hello, Jack," he said fondly. His face broke into the warmest smile Jack had ever seen. This was surely not the cold, standoffish grandfather who had raised him. Though he was older than Jack, he was still younger than when Jack last saw him, but with a caring demeanor that threw Jack off balance.

"You're the Healer?" he whispered. The older man smiled for a brief moment, then his gaze settled on Aria and his face turned to a frown.

"Bring her to the bed."

Jack did as he was instructed and laid Aria on the small bed, wet clothes and all. Jack's grandfather picked up a wooden bowl of water and dipped a rag into it.

"Bring me the brown bottle from that shelf,"

he instructed as he moved to Aria's side. Jack stood, biting back his tongue against the million questions racing through his mind. His grandfather was dead. How was he here? Had Jack died when he fell onto the mirror? Was this place a sort of afterlife? Suddenly, it all made sense. The fairytale characters, the magical powers, and being reunited with his grandfather.

"You're not dead," Grandfather said firmly, as if he were able to read Jack's mind. Jack returned with the bottle and held it out with a shaking hand.

"But you are," he whispered back, eyes wide. Without responding, the man ripped the linen to expose Aria's shoulder. Then he took the bottle from Jack, unstoppered it, and poured a golden liquid over her wound. "What is that?" Jack asked, edging closer.

"Elderflower," Grandfather mumbled. Then he glanced at Jack and shrugged. "Not the same flower you know back home. Here, it has strong healing properties."

"The women who found us… are they—"

"Elves? Yes."

A silence followed as Grandfather mopped Aria's forehead with the damp rag and tutted.

"We need to keep her body temperature down, otherwise the tonic won't do its job." He handed Jack the dripping rag.

"How is this possible?" He watched his grandfather intently. "I didn't bury an empty coffin."

"I know."

"Then how can you be here, and yet…"

"I haven't returned to England yet," Grandfather explained. "But when I do…" He turned to look at Jack. "You will still be a baby."

Jack looked at his grandfather in puzzlement. "I don't understand."

"When I left to come here, you had just been born. So, when I return…it will be as if only moments passed."

"Wait…" The thought suddenly came to Jack. "You're The Intruder? The one who rumpled everyone's stories?" Jack asked as he dabbed Aria's face.

Grandfather sat in the chair behind his desk and sighed. "That was a mistake. I was only meant to come here for a day. But alas, I could not go back." He poured a drink and looked at the rows of books as if hoping for inspiration. "When I recognized the fairy tale characters, I thought I could help them avoid some of the suffering as written in the books. But just one small change can have a ripple effect. The elves have taught me that."

"The mirror. It's elven, right?" Jack asked. Grandfather looked at him, startled, and a glimmer of pride crossed his face as he gave him a nod.

"The elves are a peaceful folk. They are wise and have means to see into the future. But they have a saying that I have learned to live by."

Jack leaned forward, clinging to his grandfather's every word. "What is that?"

Grandfather took a swig of his drink. "All things must be."

Aria stirred. Jack dipped the rag into the water again, then squeezed out the excess liquid before patting her neck.

"So, they don't interfere, at all?" Jack asked. "Then why did they help me?"

"They were helping *her*. Because it was foretold that they would," Grandfather said, nodding to Aria. Jack frowned.

"They've seen Aria's future? Does she have a book as well?"

"You aren't asking the right questions, Jack."

Jack was taken aback by yet another lesson.

"Fine. Then why did you keep the mirror a secret from me? And when raising me, why did you have to be so cold and distant all my life?"

Grandfather looked at Jack in surprise. "Raising you?"

"Yes, you raised me after my parents died."

Grandfather pinched the bridge of his nose. "Jack, I have not yet lived through that. When I left, your parents were well."

"But—"

"But nothing. You cannot tell me any more about my future. All things must be," Grandfather repeated as he pointed at Jack.

They stared at each other in silence for a moment, and Jack frowned. Was he not even sorry for everything he put him through? The lonely days, surrounded by dusty old books. Forbidding him from making friends or going to school. Only sending him on trips to camp in the outdoors, hike up mountains and sleep in a tent during a rainstorm. But Aria's heavy breathing pulled Jack back out of his mind.

He looked at her face and swept her dark hair away from her temples, and his heart warmed. All of his thoughts and worries melted away and

Grandfather seemed to know it. He chuckled and gave Jack a knowing look.

"You have many questions. And I will endeavor to answer all of them. But right now, you need to rest. You two have been through quite an ordeal, I gather." He walked over and placed a hand on Jack's shoulder. The warmth of his touch sent a rush of emotions flooding his whole body, and it took every ounce of his control not to weep.

"I can't believe you're here," Jack said in a strangled voice.

Grandfather took the rag from Jack's hand and sighed. "I know. Ah, the fire is almost out. There's a woodshed outside—would you?" He gestured to the door and Jack nodded, rising to his feet.

"Of course, I'll be right back," he said. He strode to the doorway and glanced back at Aria as she slept, his grandfather gently dabbing her face. His heart squeezed so tightly, he worried it would burst out of his chest. Aria was going to be okay, and his grandfather was not dead. All was well.

He couldn't stop the grin from overtaking his face as he marched outside and headed for the small woodshed sitting to the side. *Perhaps, this was my happy ending?* he thought. Then, as he opened the doors, something hard struck him on the back of his head, and he fell to the ground.

A pair of black boots from The Queen's men appeared inches from his face. "Aria," he croaked as he passed out.

ARIA

*A*ria jolted awake, a damp cloth falling from her forehead. She blinked several times, trying to recognize where she was.

"Oh, good. You're awake." An elven woman in a white cloak smiled as she brought a tray with hot soup.

Aria stretched out her hand and the woman's body froze on the spot, though not her face. The tray fell from her hands, dropping to the floor with a loud clang.

"I'm sorry to have startled you," the woman said, though still not able to move her body. "I just thought you would be hungry when you woke up."

Aria thought about replying, but she was too

busy looking at her own hands. Her powers were back, and stronger than ever. But then she winced as her wound stung.

She touched her shoulder. It was bandaged. *Who had done this?* She looked at the woman again. "Where's Jack?" she asked.

"He went to get some more wood for the fire," a man's voice came from the door, and Aria swung around in a defensive position.

A gray-haired man raised his hands in surrender. "There's no need for that."

"Who are you?" she asked, keeping only her good arm in front of her. "And where is Jack?"

"My grandson is fine," he said with a smile.

"Grandson?" Aria echoed, giving the man a skeptical look. "His grandfather died."

"Yes, I'm aware of that now," he replied, motioning to the frozen woman. "Would you mind letting her go? I asked her to come and help me treat you. She changed your clothes and made you some food."

Aria finally noticed the different clothes: a pair of light gray pants and a white shirt, then she glanced at the food that had fallen on the floor. Her stomach growled and she wished she hadn't been so hasty.

Without another word, she waved her good hand toward the elven woman and the ice melted.

"Thank you." The woman flashed Aria a grateful smile, though she was shivering. "Would you like me to make you another plate?"

Aria gave the woman a quizzical look. Why was she being so nice? It creeped Aria out. "Nah, that's okay."

The woman bowed then headed out the door. "Everything is ready, sir," she whispered before leaving, and the older man gave her a thankful nod.

Aria scanned the room again. Where was she? But the more pressing question was another. "Who are you, really?"

"I'm Jack's grandfather," he answered, coming to sit on a chair next to the bed.

Aria crawled away from him.

"I came through the mirror many years ago."

"Then how could you have raised him?"

"Though I have not yet returned to my land, I will," he explained, "And when I do, I will continue my life where I left off."

Aria shook her head, confused. "What do you mean where you left off?" she asked.

"When I left, my daughter was a young

mother and Jack was still a baby. So, when I go back… I will return to that time."

Aria wondered if he knew of his daughter's passing, but decided it wasn't her place. If Jack wanted him to know, he would surely share it. "Why are you telling me this?"

"Because I need your help."

Aria wanted to laugh. "What could I possibly help you with?"

"We can't let Jack go back to England."

"What?" Aria felt a sting of betrayal. How could she ask Jack to stay? Not that she hadn't thought about it, but she was leaving too. "Why would I do that?"

"Because he belongs here."

"What do you mean he belongs here?"

"His grandmother came to my world… through the mirror," he explained. "She stayed with me and we got married. But when she fell ill, she asked that her ashes be scattered on her parents' grave. That's why I came here."

"So, she was from the Chanted Kingdom?" Aria muttered, and the old man nodded. She narrowed her eyes, battling with the nagging feeling that there was more he wasn't letting on. "Then why did you keep all this from him?"

"Because I can't interfere with his story," he said.

Aria's eyes widened. "He has a story?" Then something in her brain clicked. "You're The Intruder."

The old man nodded. "And I have learned the hard way that even the most honorable of intentions can have catastrophic consequences."

"Why did you rumple everyone's lives?" Aria asked, shocked.

"I never meant to," he confessed. "I was simply trying to help. But all it took was changing one thing, and the ripple effect was pure disaster."

"So… is that why you need Jack to stay?" she asked. "To restore the happy endings to their original fate?"

The man shook his head. "Jack won't be the one to fix it," he said. "You will." He reached into her bag on top of the nightstand and pulled out the shard. Aria wanted to lunge at him and snatch her bag from his hands, then demand that he explain what he meant by *her* fixing the happy endings. But she was too curious to know what he knew about the mirror.

"This is truly one of the most extraordinary inventions of the elves," he muttered, staring at the shard as if it were a picture of an old friend. "I tried collecting all the shards once."

Aria lowered her guarded hand and edged forward. "Did you get to?"

"No." He looked up to meet her eyes. "I even tried asking the elves to make another, but they vowed to never recreate such a powerful object. In fact, they were planning on taking it high up in the sky and shattering it, but…" The man chuckled as if he was the only one in on the joke. "That would've been a bad idea."

"So, you want my mirror?" Aria asked, glancing at the shard he was still holding. "Is that how you get back home?"

"Yes." He nodded. "But I won't leave without first making sure my grandson will be cared for."

"I thought you couldn't interfere."

"I can't. That is why I'm making sure to do everything just as it's supposed to be. As hard as it may seem."

"And what is that, exactly?" she asked.

"You will find out soon enough. Now…" He stood, and Aria perked up. He was still holding her shard, and she would not allow it out of her sight. "Shall we?"

Before Aria could reply, he turned around and

walked across the room. Aria stood and followed slowly after him. He reached for a curtain and pushed it aside, revealing the Mirror of Reason with only one shard left to be completed.

Aria gasped. "My mirror!"

He stepped away, allowing her to stand protectively in front of it. "How did you get it?"

"I hired someone to get it from your hiding place," he said with a shrug. "But what's important is that it's here. And moments away from being completed." He handed the last shard to Aria, and she took it.

He raised his hands and took another step back. The extra distance eased her sudden tension. "You said I would be the one to help restore the happy endings…" she reminded him. "How could that be if I'm leaving to another world?"

"And what world is that?" he asked, more amused than curious.

"Well, the United Kingdom, of course. A place where everyone lives in peace."

The old man laughed, and she frowned. "The point is…" she cut him off, annoyed. "I'm not staying. So, you're gonna need to find someone else to clean up your mess."

"The choice is certainly yours."

"And I've already decided," she said firmly. "There is nothing for me here."

The man nodded. "Then go ahead," he said, motioning toward the mirror. "Put in the last piece."

Aria gulped, beads of sweat suddenly forming on her forehead. "I will. As soon as Jack comes back."

"He's not coming back."

His words sent an icy chill down her spine, and she peered into his strangely calm eyes. "What are you saying?"

"I'm saying…" He motioned to the mirror again. "Complete the mirror and see for yourself."

Aria turned around and pushed the shard into the empty space in the center, then hovered her finger over the gaps, filling them with ice. Once the last shard was fused, the outer frame of the mirror began to glow a bright light, and Aria stepped back, covering her eyes from the blinding glare.

"Open your eyes," the old man said, and she did. Though the golden frame was still glowing, it had dimmed slightly. She shifted her attention to the mirror. It was still cracked, merged only by her ice particles. Her reflection was slightly distorted, but she could still see her blue eyes and blonde hair as it cascaded over her injured shoulder.

"You know something else that's special about this mirror?" he asked, coming to stand behind her. When she looked at his reflection, he had white hair. "If you just ask… it will show you."

Aria's stomach twisted as she thought about what he wanted her to ask. "Mirror…" Her voice shook. "Show me Jack."

Her reflection vanished and Jack's face appeared behind a set of iron bars, and she gasped. Two guards stood to the side, and she recognized their uniform. They were The Queen's men.

The vision faded and the mirror returned to her reflection. "No!" She grabbed onto the outer frame with her eyes wide in panic. "Mirror. Show me Jack again!" When nothing happened, she demanded a third time.

"Shocking, isn't it?" the old man said, and she turned to face him with the darkest glare she could muster.

"Why?" she asked through gritted teeth.

"Why did you give him up to The Queen? The bounty on *my* head was worth a lot more than him."

He took a seat on the bed then looked up to meet her eyes. "Why I did it is not important. The real question is… what are *you* going to do?"

Aria clenched her fists. "You know if I go through that cracked mirror, I will be stuck for seven years."

"It appears you have an important choice to make." He stood and took in a deep breath. "Will you run away and save yourself? Or will you finally face The Queen and save Jack?"

JACK

*J*ack woke up on a moldy old bed. A
steady dripping in the distance
echoed and the mildew aroma
burned his nostrils. His head thumped and he sat
up with a groan. Before he could take in his
surroundings, an iron door swung open at the end
of the dark hall with a squeal, and the sound of
footsteps descended a set of stone steps to the
side.

"Oh good. You're awake."

Jack shot up to his feet and sucked in the
damp air through his teeth at the sight of a tall
woman with fiery red hair appearing before him.
A set of iron bars separated them, and even
though the cell had only a little light peeking in

through the cracks in the walls, Jack could not mistake the woman. Her long dress was made of fine silks, and a blue shawl draped over her broad shoulders. No one in this land looked so rich and powerful, and the pebble-sized jewels that adorned her fingers gleamed at him. Jack set his jaw and gave her an angry scowl.

The Queen.

"Where's Aria?"

"Aria?" She seemed surprised. "That stinking old man had Aria, too?"

Hearing her mention his grandfather sent a chill down his spine, and Jack grabbed onto the bars. "What did you do to him, you evil queen?"

The Queen raised her perfectly shaped brows and smiled serenely as she looked at Jack like a cat toying with a ball of wool.

"I see I need no introduction. But honestly, darling, I much prefer Your Majesty."

Fury raged like a storm within Jack as he glowered back at her. The woman flashed a Cheshire Cat grin, her teeth shining white in the darkness. The motion only increased Jack's anger. Though it didn't seem like she had gotten to Aria, he was still worried about his grandfather.

"You let me out, or I'll—"

"You'll what—throw a tantrum?" The Queen laughed in a high-pitched giggle that sent chills down Jack's spine. She clearly didn't see him as a threat. *But she should*, Jack thought. Once he worked out how to get out of the cell, he was going to… He couldn't finish the thought. Jack wasn't strong or powerful. He didn't even belong in this world. The frustration unhinged his anger, and he growled as he slammed his fist against the iron bars with such ferocity that The Queen's dropped.

Tiny snowflakes floated down from the damp ceiling and fell at their feet. The Queen's eyes widened as she looked at them and held out a hand, watching the snowflakes fall and melt onto her skin.

"Interesting," she said with a hum. She shook her head, as if to come out of a trance, and snapped her fingers. "You look like you could eat a horse. How about we get you cleaned up and we can talk over dinner?"

Jack stared blankly at The Queen as a guard stepped out from behind her with a set of keys jingling in his hands. The iron cell door clicked and swung open, sending a gust of chilly air.

"I look forward to our little chat. I do believe

it will be rather *illuminating*." The Queen gave him another grin before she picked up her skirts and walked out.

Jack was taken upstairs with a guard on each side. Their boots thudded against the stone floors, and Jack noticed they had been shined so much that he could see his own reflection. Huge tapestries lined the walls, picturing scenes of dragons and mountains. The sun had fully risen now, and its beams flooded the castle through tall windows. Jack squinted as they rounded a corner and he was pushed into a small room. A tin bath sat in the center of the room, filled with steaming water. And a pile of royal attire sat on a wooden stool to the side, and Jack wondered if it had belonged to George.

"We will take you to The Queen when you are dressed. And don't go thinking about running. We'll be standing outside the door." One of the guards nudged Jack on the shoulder before closing the wooden door with a bang.

Dipping into a hot bath never felt so luxurious. Since he arrived in the Chanted Forest, he only had lakes to bathe in. Jack took a bar of soap and scrubbed every inch of his aching body and toweled off absent-mindedly. He was tired. Bone tired. Ever since he fell through the mirror, he couldn't remember a time he had been able to slow down and relax.

But the relaxation was short-lived. As he dressed in royal attire and tucked his shirt in, a knock on the door made him jump.

"Do not keep The Queen waiting," one of the guards barked through the door.

Jack combed his hair and rubbed the back of his neck with a sigh. It made sense for him to be thrown in a cell, but dinner with The Queen? To what did he owe this honor? His stomach knotted and he wondered how he could play this situation to his advantage. Could The Queen have been lying about not knowing where Aria was? After all, she wouldn't give up on such a powerful weapon. And what about his grandfather? Had she any use for him at all? Or did she want to kill him just like Robin did?

He shook the thoughts away as he followed the guards down the hall. Now was not the time to dwell on such upsetting thoughts. He needed to be careful, alert, and on the lookout for every opportunity to get answers.

"My goodness, don't you scrub up well?" The Queen sat at the head of a long oak table laden with all manner of food. "Please, take a seat and help yourself."

Jack was starving and he was glad to have something other than stale bread. He silently ate a bit of everything. The sweetness of the berries was almost too rich for his palette. His stomach moaned with delight at the salty pork, and he downed the food with a cup of hot cocoa. Its velvety texture soothed his soul as he swallowed. The Queen did not eat, but merely watched in silence, an eerie smile plastered on her painted face.

"Try the apple pie. It's quite delightful."

Jack stopped, suddenly struck by a thought, and dropped his hands.

"It's poisoned," he said in horror. The Queen threw her head back and cackled.

"Good grief, why would I poison you?" She stroked her red hair and raised her chalice to her lips.

"Why would you bring me here? What use am I to you?" Jack asked, his blood turning cold. Something felt off, but he couldn't put his finger on what.

"I have eyes and ears in all of the forest, and it sounds like you've been quite a busy bee," the queen explained after she took a sip of her drink. "I was told that you have been running around with my princess."

Jack balled his hands and set his jaw, but The Queen continued unaware.

"You evaded my guards, outsmarted an ogre, survived the wrath of Robin Hood, and you befriended a mermaid. Not to mention caused two ships to sink."

Jack frowned. Why did The Queen make him sound so heroic?

"Tell me, Jack, how long have you known you had powers?"

The question threw him off guard. "What? I don't have powers," he said.

The Queen cocked a brow and raised her chalice—an elaborate golden goblet covered in ice crystals. Then she set it down. "I am told you know about the stories—the *fairy tales*, as I believe you call them. You know about the future."

Jack shook his head. "It's not like that. Everything is different."

"Thanks to the Intruder, I know." She nodded. "But that only tells me these stories can be rewritten."

Jack clamped his hands over his knees and stared at her. "Why do you want to do that?"

"Jack, my darling. I want to offer you a role. A very special position here at my court." The Queen rose to her feet and walked to him.

"What kind of position?"

"An advisor. I need you to tell me about these happy endings."

She planted a hand on his shoulder, and he stiffened. "Well, I can't tell for sure. There are a lot of evil queens in the old books."

The Queen's smile faded for a moment, but she grinned at him again as she gave his shoulder a squeeze. "Evil. Oh please, you make me sound like I'm a—"

"Cold-blooded murderer," Jack said acidly as he gripped the table.

"Careful," The Queen said, eyeing the wood as it turned into a block of ice. "If you want to hurt me, you should know that I have protection. Whoever kills me... dies."

Jack stared and blinked at her, incredulously.

"Besides, I thought you didn't mind. Seeing as you've chosen to spend all your time with a killer." The Queen's expression grew dark. "And soon I'm going to—"

"Don't hurt Aria," Jack blurted out. He sounded far too pleading, but just saying her name had his resolve breaking. He cleared his throat. "If you want to find your happy ending, you need to let her go. Not use her."

The Queen laughed again, prompting Jack to recoil inwardly. "My happy ending? Is that what you think I want? Oh, Jack…"

"What do you want, then?" he asked.

"I want to know how they defeat me, so I can stop them." Her smile grew even darker. "Well, I guess that would be my happy ending after all, now wouldn't it?"

"And why would I help you do that?"

She crouched down to sit eye-level with him and batted her lashes. "If you agree to be my advisor, I will stop burning down villages. And I'll leave the ice princess to run around my kingdom in safety."

"You'll stop the killing? And leave Aria alone?" Jack asked, his stomach churning. He didn't like how close The Queen's face sat away from his own. "What about my grandfather? What did you do to him?"

"The old man is fine," she assured him. "After all, he kept his end of the deal."

"What deal?"

The Queen flashed an amused smile. "Why, to hand you over to me, of course. How do you think you ended up here?"

Jack stared at her with eyes unblinking. His grandfather had betrayed him. But why?

"So, what will it be Jack?" The Queen pressed, and Jack turned to meet her eyes.

"You'll really leave Aria alone?"

"I promise not to touch a wisp of blonde hair on her pretty head," she said simply, holding her hand over her heart. Jack chewed his lip in thought.

"Okay then."

The Queen's eyes widened in surprise.

"You mentioned Robin Hood before. I can tell you how he's going to defeat King Richard," he said, and The Queen looked like the cat who got the cream.

"Does this mean you accept my offer?" she asked, her eyes wide and hopeful.

Jack set his jaw and studied her for a moment. If this stopped anyone else from getting hurt, and gave Aria a chance at freedom, how could he not?

"Yes." He sucked in a deep breath. "I'll work for you."

ARIA

"*Y*es." Aria watched Jack through the mirror. *"I'll work for you."*

The vision vanished, and she grabbed onto the brass frame so hard, it turned to ice. "She's going to use him as a weapon," she whispered in disbelief. And how had Aria not noticed that Jack had powers?

"That was supposed to have been you," the old man said from across the room, and Aria swung around with a sharp glare.

"It wasn't supposed to be either of us," she spoke through gritted teeth. "How could you betray your own grandson?"

"I only did what had to be done——" A blast of ice hit his chest and threw him back. Before he could regain his balance, Aria had him pinned to the wall, ice traveling from her hands onto his body.

"If you kill me, it will alter Jack's entire childhood," he warned.

"A life without you in it?" She chuckled despite the anger boiling in her veins. "Now, that doesn't sound so bad."

"If I'm not there to raise him when his parents die, then he will be sent to a home away from the manor." He locked his gray eyes with hers. "Away from the *mirror*. Which means he would never have come here."

"You're a cold-hearted monster," she hissed.

He frowned. "Oh, you have no idea."

She looked at him in confusion, then pressed a hand over his chest, sensing the temperature of his heart. Her eyes widened in surprise as she looked up at him again. "Your heart is frozen."

He cocked his head. "What happened to my heart isn't relevant right now. What matters now is Jack."

Aria shook her head, her thoughts spinning. "That's why you were so cold and distant to Jack growing up. Now it makes sense why he was raised without warmth and love."

"The love is there," he said firmly. "It's just not clouded by emotions."

Aria looked at his stone-cold expression. Even when he talked about love, he conveyed nothing. No emotion. She shook her head again then turned to look at the mirror for the thousandth time.

Though all she could see was her reflection, her mind was still stuck on the last image she'd seen of Jack. She had so much to apologize for. But most importantly, so much more to own up to.

She clenched her fists and glared at her own reflection. The girl staring back at her had been nothing but a coward. And now the kindest boy she'd ever known was taking her place under the claws of a monster.

"How does this work?" she asked, hating that she still needed the old man's help. She'd never crossed through the mirror before, and she couldn't afford to waste any more time. She needed to rescue Jack.

"Just *think* about where you want to go," he said. "And hold your breath."

Aria touched the mirror, and it began to glow as if reflecting a bright star. She sucked in a breath while images of Jack flooded her mind. The glass then turned into a thick, silver liquid, and she held her breath as she stepped inside.

———

*A*ria was deep underwater, and her injured shoulder stung as she swam to the surface.

Once she reached the top, she gasped for air. The Queen's castle towered above her and she realized she was in the castle's lake.

"Who's there?" a guard called out from behind her. She whipped around, only to see her reflection on the icy wall. Her blonde hair glistened brightly in the sun, and there was no more hiding the princess.

Before the guard could say another word, she stretched out her hand and threw him back with a blast of ice. He dropped to the ground, unconscious. Her shoulder burned, and she bit back the pain caused by the surge of power that came out of her.

With her shoulder still injured, she swam to the edge with her good arm, then crawled out of the lake. She thought about hiding the guard by pushing him into the lake and let him drown, but then Jack's disapproving look surfaced from the back of her mind and she rolled her eyes.

"Fine…" she grumbled to the Jack inside her head. "I'll try not to kill anyone."

Ignoring the throbbing in her wound, she lifted the guard's limp body and dragged him behind the nearest bush. After taking his sword and his helmet which covered her face, she stripped him out of his uniform and put it on herself. It was large on her petite frame, but it would have to do.

As soon as she stepped inside the castle, the scent of lavender washed over her, flooding her mind with childhood memories. Her heart tightened in her chest, and she leaned against the wall, biting back tears as memories of her and her sister playing in those halls rushed back to her mind.

Two guards appeared around the corner, and Aria stood up straight. They greeted her with a slight nod as they walked past, and Aria let out a long breath of relief when they disappeared from sight. But when she noticed more guards coming, she rushed into the kitchen.

The laughter of the women as they cleaned

the dirty dishes lifted Aria's heart a little, reminding her of the many times the maids would sneak her a piece of chocolate before supper.

As soon as one of the servants noticed Aria standing there, she cleared her throat to signal the rest to stop talking. The lively chatter died to a deafening silence, but it was the frightened expression on the women's faces that filled Aria with concern.

Why were they so afraid?

"May we help you?" one of the women asked while keeping her head down to avoid eye contact.

Aria cleared her throat and deepened her voice since she was still disguised in a guard's uniform. "I'm looking for The Queen's new advisor, Jack."

Before any of the women could answer, another guard stepped in from the back door with his helmet on and scanned around the room. "You." He pointed to a young maid in the corner with glossy black braids. "You're needed outside." He stepped aside to allow the young maid to walk past him.

The girl kept her head down as she walked out the back door, but when the guard followed after her, it sent a chill down Aria's spine. Something wasn't right.

What were these guards doing to the women?

Aria stepped forward but was blocked by an older woman. Her face looked familiar. She had been the girls' handmaid growing up. It had only been a year, but she had aged so much.

"I can take you to the new advisor," the woman offered, and a warm feeling rose in Aria as she heard her handmaid's voice after all this time. The dragon-slaying bedtime stories she used to read to Aria after her sister fell asleep surfaced in her mind. But Aria shook off the feeling and looked toward the back door again.

"Who was that young woman?" Aria asked, her voice deep.

"My niece, sir."

No wonder her voice was shaky. As much as Aria needed to get to Jack, she felt a strong pull to save her maid's niece from the clutches of that guard.

Aria walked around the woman and hurried out the back door. She looked to the right and spotted the guard leading the young woman into a plant tunnel near the garden.

Oh, no you're not.

Aria rushed after them, and by the time she rounded the corner, he already had the young woman pinned against the flowery arch.

"Step away from the girl," Aria demanded, drawing her sword. When the guard didn't move, Aria took another step toward them. "I said... back away from the girl."

The guard turned around, drawing his sword and swinging at Aria. The young maid screamed as Aria blocked his blade with a loud *clang*. She jumped back, giving herself more room to move. Her shoulder ached, but adrenaline coursed through her veins.

"Get out of here!" Aria said to the girl as the guard came at her again. She blocked his blows a second and third time. He was agile and skilled, but even with one good arm, she was still a better fighter. She grazed his hand, and when he dropped his sword, she kicked him in the stomach. As soon as he fell back, his helmet flew off and she towered over him, pushing her blade to his neck.

But then he looked up and their eyes met. "George?"

He kicked her leg, and she fell, her back slamming against the grass. She grimaced at the impact on her shoulder. The pain was so excruci-ating, it made her stomach churn.

"George, please don't," the young maid pleaded. *Why hasn't she run away?*

"I have to kill him," George said. "Otherwise, he could tell my mother you're alive."

Aria opened her eyes only to find George raising his sword over her.

"Wait…" Aria winced as she lifted her hand. The sword turned to ice and he jumped back, startled. The wave of shock that washed through him gave Aria just enough time to pull her helmet off and look up at him.

"Aria?" he whispered in disbelief, and Aria flashed him a pained smile.

"Aria?" The young maid stepped out of the shadow, and when the orange light of the sunset illuminated her face, Aria gasped.

"Snow?"

"Aria!"

Her younger sister ran to her, then dropped to her knees and wrapped her arms around Aria's neck. Her shoulder ached, but she didn't care. Her sister was alive.

"How did you…?" Aria's voice shook as she pushed back the tears. "I thought you were dead."

"A dwarf hid me," Snow explained, her voice muffled from having her face buried in Aria's neck. Aria only knew of one dwarf in the castle, the gardener. "He saved me from the fire then kept me hidden here, in the castle."

"What about our parents?" Aria asked, running her fingers through her sister's soft braid. "Are they…?"

Snow pulled back, crying, and shook her head. Aria wiped the tears from her sister's porcelain cheeks. "Why didn't you leave this place?"

"I'm not like you, Aria," she said, tears still sliding down her face. "I wouldn't know how to survive out there. I thought about going to the dwarf village, but…" Snow's expression fell, and Aria wiped her sister's tears. Just as she used to when they were young. Though at sixteen, she still needed her big sister to comfort her.

"The Queen burned it down. I know."

"I've been okay here," Snow assured her. "The maids have all been looking out for me. They bring me food." She smiled. "They even dyed my hair black so I fit in with them. And ever since George woke up… he's been looking after me, too."

George came to crouch next to Snow and

Aria flashed him a smile. "It's so good to see you. But how did you…?"

"My mother thawed me after she'd conquered the kingdom," he said with a frown. "But I haven't said anything to her about Snow. Your sister has been safe here with me." When he glanced at Snow and her porcelain cheeks turned red, Aria suddenly realized that was the same reaction she'd always had around George.

Aria touched her sister's flushed cheeks. "Why didn't you tell me you were in love with him? You know I would've never gone through with the wedding if I knew."

"I know." She looked at George and held his gaze for a long moment. "But we agreed that it was best for the kingdom."

"You agreed?" Aria punched George in the chest, and he stumbled backward. "And here I thought *I* was making the sacrifice."

"There she is!" a guard yelled from the end of the plant tunnel, followed by more guards. "Get the princess!"

Aria jumped to her feet and kicked up her sword.

"This way!" George called out, but as they

followed him, more guards appeared on the other end, trapping them in the tunnel.

"I know another way!" Snow called out, cutting through the arch with George's sword and running across the garden.

As they reached the willow tree, she kicked away the snow covering an iron door on the ground. George reached for the latch and pulled it open.

Aria helped her sister down a ladder then followed after her. Snow grabbed a torch from the wall with the fire still burning and waited for George to close and lock the latch.

"What is this place?" George asked once his feet found the ground. Snow pointed the torch toward the dark hall.

"It's an underground tunnel that leads to different areas of the castle," Snow explained, starting down the dark hallway. "This way will take us right to the woods outside the walls."

"I remember this tunnel," Aria said, her heart squeezing at the memory. "Father took me this way *that* night. Then he told me to run and never look back."

When they turned the last corner, the tunnel came to an end, leading into the woods. The blue sky had darkened to an indigo color and Aria turned to George.

"Walk that trail to the end," she said, pointing into the woods. "Then follow the signs to Sherwood Forest. Find Robin Hood. He will help you."

"Wait, you're not coming?" Snow asked.

Aria pulled her sister into a hug. "I'll be right behind you," she promised as more snowflakes fell from the sky. "But I need to go back for Jack."

JACK

*J*ack's heart panged as Aria's face flooded his mind. Would he ever see her again? And why had his grandfather betrayed him?

He tugged on his shirt collar and bent his legs to loosen his pants, yet they continued to cling to him like a second skin. He caught his reflection in a mirror and eyed the red jacket with gold stitching. At a glance, he looked like a prince. He straightened his spine and stuck his thumbs in his pockets. Was this his life now? To be a royal advisor to The Evil Queen? He boggled over how he ended up in this predicament.

And his *powers*?

He looked at his hands. How had he not

noticed before? How the freezing waters at Pirate Cove didn't feel cold to him. Or the supernatural winds howling inside Belle's manor. It couldn't have been Aria because her powers were suppressed by the bracelet at that time. It was him. He'd done all those things.

How could he return home to that boring world?

Perhaps he could make a difference in this kingdom? No one was waiting for him to return to the manor, except his family lawyer. Which was a disappointing thought. Maybe he could find purpose in the Chanted Kingdom and use his powers for good? There had been so much devastation, so much tragedy. What if he could convince The Queen to rule peacefully and guide her away from violence?

Ironically, a commotion outside interrupted his thoughts. He bolted out of the room and hurried down the hall, following the sound of screeching and crashes.

"You killed thousands of innocent lives! Did you really think I wouldn't want to make you pay?"

The angry shout made Jack's heart leap. He recognized that feisty voice.

Aria.

But what was she doing here? The Queen had promised him she wouldn't go after her.

He dashed out to the gardens. The clouds darkened in the sky and there was a chill in the air. But he didn't notice. He stared wide-eyed at Aria and The Queen screeching at each other, the lake sitting between them with a fountain to the side.

"Aria!" Jack rushed forward, and The Queen directed a hard look at him.

"Seize him," she commanded. Two burly guards roughly grasped Jack's arms. Their grip tightened the more he wrestled against them.

"Let me go!"

Aria raised her hands and the fountain spray turned into icicles. She then hurtled them toward The Queen, who in return disappeared in a fiery blaze. The icicles melted as they crashed with the heat, dripping like rain yet never reaching the ground before evaporating with a hiss.

The Queen reappeared across the lake with a fiery glare toward Aria. And when she stepped forward, her skin became shimmering scales while her teeth grew into fangs. It took several seconds for Jack's brain to process what he was seeing. He blinked hard and stared open-mouthed at a dragon, bearing down and spewing fire toward Aria. The red of the dragon's scales glistered and it had claws the size of swords.

Aria crouched behind a tall tree, which turned black on one side and blew away as ashes in the wind. The dragon crawled around, its wings flexing and nose snorting smoke. The smell was overpowering and the smoke stung Jack's eyes.

"Look who's showing their true colors!" Aria shouted as she looked up at the flying creature. "No going back now, Your Majesty. Everyone knows what a monster you really are!"

Jack craned his neck to see the castle windows were filled with shocked faces, though the guards keeping him in their grasp remained serious and unfazed.

Suddenly, it all made sense. This was how the villages had been burned down so completely. Whenever The Queen got hot-tempered, all she needed to do was turn into a dragon, fly over a village, and spew. *Talk about letting off steam*, Jack thought.

Aria pulled out her knife and ran around the opposite side of the fountain, scurrying unnoticed between the dragon's legs. Its mammoth head swung left and right, its yellow eyes darting around as it looked for Aria.

Jack's heart dropped as he watched Aria bury her knife in the dragon's belly. The dragon roared up to the sky. A blast of fire shot upwards and then the dragon looked down and gripped Aria in its claws. She cried out in pain and her knife fell with a clatter to the ground.

Jack's stomach lurched and he grunted as he tried to break free from the guards, watching Aria struggle. But then the dragon whimpered and staggered back, its claws frozen solid. Aria squatted and retrieved her knife then rose and stepped away from the wounded dragon, her chest heaving. For a beat, nothing happened. It was as if both parties were too tired to continue.

But then the dragon snorted at its claws and the ice melted. Then, as quick as a flash, the dragon's huge tail swiped Aria, throwing her off her feet, and she fell with a thud to the ground. Jack clamped his jaw and glared at the guards standing by him.

"How can you stand by and watch this? She's your princess."

"Shut up, fool. We only follow The Queen's orders," one of them muttered, squeezing Jack's bicep. A sprinkle of snowflakes began falling from the sky as Jack gave him a steely look.

"Your queen is a dragon, so what threat am I? Just let me go." The guards ignored him, and Jack's muscles tensed as anger boiled in his chest. He looked back to see Aria shooting ice out of her hands, but it melted as the dragon roared back. Aria stumbled, throwing her hands out, but less ice appeared than before. She was growing weaker, and blood was seeping from her shoulder wound.

Suddenly, Jack remembered what The Queen had said about her protection, and it jolted all his senses.

If Aria slays the dragon, she'll die. But if she doesn't slay the dragon, she'll still die.

Neither of those outcomes was acceptable.

The dragon stretched its wings out wide and flapped them, sending a thunderous wind over the garden. Trees swayed violently and the falling snow shot to the side like a blizzard. Jack furrowed his brows and focused. The snow immediately responded and moved at his will, encircling the dragon in an icy tornado.

Aria staggered forward, her knife held out in a shaking hand, and the dragon broke away from the tornado with a deadly roar. Aria jumped out of the way just in time as a blast of fire shot past, but she cried out again as she fell. This time, she did not get back up. This was it. Jack had to do something. He couldn't just stand and watch Aria die.

He shut his eyes and homed in on the avalanche within his chest. He imagined it growing larger and larger, until his body could not possibly contain it any longer. Every molecule of his being buzzed, and when he opened his eyes, everything looked bright, as if his sight had been dramatically improved. He opened his mouth and let out a tremendous roar, and the two guards flew back as if they had been hit by an invisible force.

Jack raised his hands and summoned a violent snowstorm. The air grew thick and freezing, and the guards shivered as they laid on the ground, their lips turning blue. Jack stooped down and grasped a sword from one of the fallen guards, then he marched through the thick blizzard. Despite the frost and wind, Jack could see perfectly. The dragon looked around, disorientated, and jets of fire hissed in the storm. Aria lay panting on the ground. When their eyes met, she looked at Jack like this was the first time she was seeing him.

But there was no time for Jack to brood on it, and for once, his brain didn't spiral into thoughts. He was more alive than ever. The wind, the snow, the ice, it was all connected to him now. And it fueled him with a confidence he had never known.

He turned away from Aria and looked at the dragon. His reflection in her eyes showed that for the first time he *was* a real threat. Looking at The Queen with a mixture of pity and coldness, he stepped closer until there was just a few feet between them.

The Queen hummed, and Jack peered at her resigned expression. A fiery tower shot up to the clouds and a mighty roar made the ground rumble. Jack waved his sword, but the dragon's tail tossed him back, casting the sword out of his hands and into the scorched bushes. Jack got up and turned to retrieve it, but the dragon roared and flames blocked his path. His heart thumped so fast he could hear the beat drumming in his ears. He swallowed and followed his gut. He needed a weapon, but he had nothing close by.

He rolled to the side to avoid another fiery

blast and mustered the snow to crystallize and harden, molding it into the finest sword he had ever seen. The weight of the handle was heavy and sat smoothly in his right hand.

He gave a final glance to Aria and nodded as if offering her a farewell. Her eyes moistened as she stared at him.

"It's all right," Jack mouthed. Then he ducked as her tail swung over his head. Jack summoned every ounce of his energy and focused on building the biggest storm he could over the dragon. The sky grew black, and the mixture of ash and snow turned the world black and white.

And suddenly, it *was* black and white. Jack knew what he had to do. It had been right there all along. Somehow, he was supposed to fall through the mirror. He needed to help Aria on her quest. He couldn't explain it in his head, yet it felt right. It was the reason why he never belonged in the manor. Why he possessed the powers to overcome a dragon. This moment was his destiny. And he knew exactly what he had to do. Whatever the cost.

Jack stepped forward, his frozen crystal sword raised, gripping the handle so tightly that his knuckles ached. No fear took up any part of his mind. And despite the chaos of the howling winds and the extinguished roars, he walked as if in slow motion, feeling clear headed. He was the embodiment of calm as he stepped into the smoke and walked to the underbelly of the beast.

He shut his eyes and pictured Aria with her long hair blonde, wearing an ice-blue gown with a sheer lace shawl draped over her shoulders. A tiara made of diamonds sat over her forehead in a V and she looked down, her dark lashes touching her cheeks. She would become queen of the Chanted Kingdom and everyone would live in peace. The thought gave him the fuel to step forward and drive the sword deep into the beast's heart.

A monstrous shriek ricocheted off the walls of the castle, followed by the squeal of a wounded animal. Jack staggered back, and the ice sword shattered into a thousand pieces, falling to the ground. The dragon slumped onto the frozen lake and exhaled its final breath.

Jack was empty. The snow stopped falling, and the dark clouds faded, giving way to the weak sunshine high in the sky. He turned and tried to smile at Aria as she stumbled toward him. But he couldn't. Instead, his knees buckled and he fell hard on his back. He felt no pain. No fear. Just peace and calm, like a cool spring morning.

"Aria," he whispered as she fell at his side and pulled his head onto her lap. Her tears landed on his cheeks, but in his peaceful state, he could not understand why she was crying. The Evil Queen had been defeated. Aria could return to her castle and take back the throne. All was well.

And with that final thought, Jack closed his eyes and took his last breath.

ARIA

"*I*t's Aria. Our young princess." The hushed whispers spread through the crowds like a wave. "The Evil Queen is dead."

Aria was barely conscious of the people gathering around her as she cradled Jack's lifeless body in her arms. "Jack…" She choked on his name. Her chest was so tight, she could barely breathe.

There was a shift in the air beside her as someone knelt down and gently placed a hand on her good shoulder. She looked up and spotted her sister with eyes full of tears. Her aching heart panged with a mixture of relief and sorrow to see her sister.

"When we saw the dragon and all the fire, we

had to come back. I'm so glad you're alive," she said, her voice shaky.

But Aria wasn't glad. She was supposed to be the one to kill The Queen and save the kingdom. All she had done was run away. She had become so wrapped up in her mission to escape, she didn't take a moment to stop and think about Jack. Until it was too late.

"He's gone, Snow!" Aria cried, her voice raspy. "He's really gone."

"He saved our kingdom," Snow whispered, and the heroic image of Jack slaying the dragon filled Aria's heart with pride. He really was a hero. *Her* hero. She focused on his peaceful face through her blurry vision, and memories of all they'd been through together flooded her mind like a beautiful dream.

She ran a hand through his soft brown hair. "I should've told him," she whispered to her sister while keeping her eyes on his peaceful face. "Now he'll never know just how much he meant to me."

"I'm sure he knew."

Aria shook her head, her heart squeezing in her chest. "You don't understand. Everything about him was kind. His thoughts... his eyes... his heart." She rested her hand over his chest, but when there was no movement, her heart ached and she broke down again. "I loved him, Snow."

Aria didn't have to look at her sister to know she was crying too. But then a wave of sorrow filled the air, and Aria looked up to find her maids with their faces buried in their hands, also weeping.

"Aria." Snow's eyes stretched wide. "I have an idea."

Aria looked into her sister's hopeful eyes. "What?"

"True love's kiss." Snow looked at George, who'd been standing across from them that whole time, then shifted her attention back to Aria. "It's the only thing more powerful than death."

Aria's shoulders sagged. "Oh, Snow… that wouldn't work with me."

"How do you know?"

"Because…" She looked at Jack again. "We don't have a story like everyone else." She mumbled the latter because she didn't expect anyone to understand.

"You could at least try…" George chimed in with a hollow voice. His face had turned ashen gray as if he was still reeling from the shock of losing his mother. "It's not like you could hurt him. And if he freezes, he'd just be preserved until the funeral."

Snow glared at him for his bluntness, but he wasn't wrong. Aria looked at Jack, a sliver of hope rising in her chest.

Could this really work?

She loved him, it was true, but did Jack love her back? The memory of him cradling her in his arms and smoothing her hair with his hand sent tears leaking out of her eyes again.

If their roles were reversed, Jack would've tried it. In fact, he would've moved heaven and Earth if it meant there was a chance to save her. She owed him that much. "Okay…" She sucked in a nervous breath and her heart began to race.

She cupped his cold cheeks with shaky hands then closed her eyes. "Come back to me, Jack," she whispered only to him then leaned in and touched her icy lips to his.

She pulled back with her heart pounding in her chest. The silence around her was deafening. Then particles of ice began to cover his lifeless body like a wave covering the shore.

Aria gasped, her eyes filling with tears as she watched the ice cover him completely. Nothing happened. She threw herself onto Snow's lap, sobbing. Her sister's arms wrapped around her so tight, as if she were trying to keep Aria together through sheer force.

Aria's heart burned as she continued to cry. Even though The Queen was gone and the kingdom would finally be restored to its rightful ruler, none of it mattered without Jack. She couldn't bear the emptiness.

"Aria..." Her sister's voice was barely above a whisper. "Look..."

Aria sat up slowly, and when her eyes landed on Jack, she gasped.

His frozen body began to glow white, the light growing stronger until she had to shield her eyes.

"Is this supposed to happen?" Aria whispered to Snow, who looked just as confused.

Aria turned back at the sound of ice splintering. A gust of cold wind encircled Jack's body and lifted him in the air. Millions of tiny ice fragments broke from his body and shattered like glass on the ground.

Aria's heart raced as she stumbled to her feet and stared at Jack, who was so bright she could barely see his face.

Snowflakes fell from the sky above Jack's body and swept around him, picking up speed, and the white glow faded just enough for Aria to see Jack's body covered in snowflakes. They fused together and sank into his skin. His muddy brown hair lightened to the purest shade of white.

The whirlwind lowered him to his feet and he opened his eyes. Aria stepped back, shaken. His eyes were gray with flecks of silver and his gaze settled on her. The snowstorm evaporated and the sun peeked through the clouds. Its rays landed on Jack. Aria hardly dared to breathe.

He'd transformed into the most beautiful being she'd ever seen. And for a long moment, there was nothing but silence.

"Aria…" Jack breathed her name, and the sweet sound of his voice sent her emotions reeling. Before he could take another breath, she leapt into his arms, and without warning, her mouth was on his. She felt his jolt of surprise, but it didn't take long before his arms were tight around her waist and he was pulling her against him. When his lips parted, a rush of ice-cold air flooded her senses, refreshing the deepest part of her soul. He kissed her back, completely unyield-ing, and an electrifying sensation spread through her so quickly, she ceased listening to her brain entirely. He lifted her up and spun her around, cinching her to him, then deepened the kiss in the most delicious way. She buried her hands in his white hair, feeling the silken strands between her fingers.

Someone cleared their throat, and Jack's lips suddenly softened as her feet found the ground. Aria pulled back with her eyes still closed, reveling in the taste of this man who had just claimed her heart.

"Jack…" His grandfather's voice came from behind the crowd, and they both turned to look. The people stepped aside to make way for the old man to approach.

"Grandfather, you're here!" Jack's face lit up, his hands still entwined with Aria's.

But Aria dropped Jack's hands and shot his grandfather a look so fierce, she was surprised icicles didn't shoot out of them.

How can he show his face here? After what he did.

She stood silently seething as Jack and his grandfather embraced, patting each other on the back. When they broke apart, his grandfather looked around at the crowds of people, still staring at them.

"Is there somewhere we can go, to have a talk?" he asked quietly. Jack looked at Aria, his face hopeful, and her heart leapt. But part of her wanted to order the guards to take the old man to the dungeons.

"Sure. This way…" she said through gritted teeth. She led them to the library. It was the quietest place in the castle, which offered them much needed privacy.

"Jack," his grandfather said softly. Aria looked up at him, startled at the tears in his eyes. They both took a seat while Aria pretended to peruse the books, looking for something to read. She got the impression this was going to be an intimate conversation, but she didn't trust the old man to be alone with Jack.

His grandfather pulled out a hand mirror from his pocket and held it out for Jack to look into. Aria tried not to stare as Jack peered into it and raised a hand through his white hair.

"Woah. I look so different," he said in awe. He glanced at Aria before he looked at his grandfather again. "I feel different too."

His grandfather handed him a small book, Jack looked down and his brows knitted together.

"Jack Frost," he said blankly. Then he looked up with wide eyes. "You're telling me…" He didn't finish, but his grandfather nodded along, following his train of thought.

"Your grandmother was from this kingdom. That is why I came here." He took out a white handkerchief and dabbed his eyes. "She wanted her ashes to be brought back to her land. But I got stuck here, and I thought I could be helpful. But I only made things worse."

Jack stood up and walked over to the window, rubbing the back of his neck. He glanced at Aria again and held out his hand. She didn't hesitate. Feeling his skin against hers was addictive. And part of her was still wondering if this was just a dream. As if reading her thoughts, Jack gave her hand a reassuring squeeze.

"I'm from here," he whispered. Then he turned to look at his grandfather again and pulled Aria to stand close to him, his arm wrapped around her waist.

"Jack," his grandfather said, rising to his feet and tears running down his face. This time he didn't even attempt to dab them away. "The reason I have been cold and distant with you all this time… I needed to prepare you to come here. And I couldn't interfere with your story. Or none of this would have happened."

Aria frowned at the sight of the old man becoming wracked with emotion.

"But did you really need to be so… sterile? I was just a child, and I had no other family. You made me feel unloved."

"My heart is frozen. I'm deeply sorry."

"Frozen?" Jack echoed. "How come?"

His grandfather smiled. "That's a story for another day."

They embraced again and his grandfather wept quietly into Jack's shoulder.

"But you have to know, I did everything for your benefit. Because I do love you. I always have." Jack's grandfather sniffed and stepped back as Jack nodded thoughtfully.

"A frozen heart. Well, I suppose I can believe that." He laughed softly. "Will you have to go back through the portal? We've only just been reunited."

His grandfather planted a hand on his cheek and smiled sadly. "If I don't, there's going to be a little boy without any family, who will never discover the mirror that will take him back to his true home."

"What else do you know about my heritage?

How can I learn more about my powers? Do I have family in this kingdom?"

Jack's grandfather nodded. "Go to the Ice Mountains. You will find answers there."

Aria swallowed uncomfortably. She had heard tales about the Ice Mountains. That they were treacherous and the few people who ventured there never returned.

Jack nodded and held the book to his heart as he shared a silent look with his grandfather. It was as if the two of them finished their conversation tele-pathically. Then his grandfather broke the silence.

"May I speak with Aria for a moment?" He put a hand on Jack's shoulder, and Jack hugged his grandfather one last time before walking out of the library. But not before he flashed Aria a smile that made her heart flutter. When he left, Aria turned to the old man.

"Why did you lie to him?" Aria asked, giving him a skeptical look. "You said your heart was still frozen, but if that were the case, your emotions wouldn't have overwhelmed you just now."

"Beautiful and smart, I see." The old man smiled. "And you are quite right. My heart thawed the moment I saw Jack die." He took a deep breath as if bracing himself for a blow. "It takes a lot to be a villain, Aria. More than we may bargain for sometimes."

"We?"

The old man watched her for a long moment, then he pulled another book out of his pocket and handed it to Aria. It was entitled *The Snow Queen*.

Aria looked up to meet his eyes again. "Is this…?"

"Your story, yes."

She looked at the book again with eyes wide. "But Jack said he never read about me."

"Oh, but he did. He just never knew who you were."

When the old man said nothing else, she finally understood what he was saying. "I'm a villain."

"You weren't always," he clarified. "But with The Queen dead, someone has to step up and take the role."

"Why?"

"Because that's how the happy endings are restored," he explained, and Aria looked up at him. "Without evil to be conquered, true love won't blossom. Princesses won't need saving. And Princes won't rescue. Take your sister, for example…" He came to stand next to Aria by the window and they both turned to look at Snow in the castle grounds. "George is not her prince charming."

"But they love each other."

"For now…" he said, his voice just as crushed as Aria's heart. "But it won't be strong enough to weather the storm because he isn't her *true* love."

"Then who is?"

"A brave soul that won't be afraid of his mother."

The old man had a point. George could have stood up to his mother all this time, but he never did. He allowed Snow to live by hiding in the castle, but never actually freed her from that prison.

"So back in your cabin, when you said I would be the one to restore the happy endings… you knew it would be like this, didn't you?" When the old man didn't respond, she turned to face him. "You knew Jack would kill The Queen, and that I would have to take her place."

"I only hoped," he confessed. "But I couldn't interfere."

"But you did."

"No, I played my part," he corrected. "It's different."

"How so?"

"If I had told you what needed to happen, *you* would have been driven to save him out of knowledge, not love. And when Jack killed The Queen, that solidified his love for you. If neither of you had made those decisions on your own, driven by love, then that kiss wouldn't have transformed him because it wouldn't have been true love's kiss."

Aria looked at the book she was still holding, and her heart squeezed. "Jack will never be okay with this."

Grandfather placed an encouraging hand on her shoulder. "You are the queen now. And being a good leader means forgoing your own happiness for the sake of your kingdom. You have the means to restore your kingdom to its purest condition, and to help your people find true love. The question then remains... how much are you willing to sacrifice?"

A tear slid down Aria's cheek and landed on the book. "Do you really think I have what it takes to follow through with this?"

"If ever you need any guidance," he said,

offering her a soft smile, "just ask the Mirror of Reason, and you shall find your answers."

Aria lifted her head and looked at the old man with eyes full of tears. "Will I lose Jack?"

He smiled, wiping away one of her tears. "You will never lose Jack. He's your true love."

She sucked in a breath then hid the book under her garment. "I guess it's time for you to go then?"

He nodded. "There is one more thing I need to ask you." He reached for Aria's hand, and she looked at him, confused. He stole a quick glance toward the door to make sure Jack hadn't returned, then placed her hand over his chest. "I need you to freeze my heart again."

"What?" Aria tried pulling her hand away, but he firmed his grip and peered into her eyes.

"Aria…" His jaw clenched as his eyes filled with tears. "I already lost my wife, and when I go back, I will lose my daughter. If I have to bear that pain, I will not be strong enough for Jack. Please…" He softened his grip, but kept his hand over hers. "Freeze my heart."

More tears slid down her face as she released her power onto his chest and into his heart. He grimaced as the ice particles hardened his heart, but within a few seconds he was able to breathe again.

Aria pulled her hand away, recoiling from what she'd done. Jack would grow up without warmth and affection, and she would be responsible for that. Again.

"Thank you," he breathed, rubbing his chest. "You will make a great evil queen. I'm certain of it."

Aria pulled him into a hug. "I will try my best." She pulled back and wiped her tears away. "How will you be getting home?"

He looked out the window and Aria followed his gaze toward the lake. "That lake, when frozen, becomes a portal."

Aria gasped.

"That's where the elves got the idea from," Grandfather added. "So, that's where I'll be going. I've also made arrangements for your mirror to be brought here. You need to keep it safe. Guard it with your life."

Aria nodded. "I will."

Once Grandfather left the library, Aria went to find Jack, who was talking with Snow and George in the hall.

"Aria!" Snow's face lit up. "He is delightful!"

Aria smiled at her sister's giddy expression. "Yes, he is."

As Aria made her way toward Jack, Snow grabbed George by the hand and pulled him away.

"Is he gone already?" Jack asked with a frown. "What did he want to talk to you about?"

Aria wrapped her arms around Jack's neck then pressed her lips to his. It was warm and sweet, and in that moment that was all that mattered. When she pulled back, he was smiling again.

"I can get used to this," he joked, but then his expression turned serious as he studied her face. "Are you okay?"

"I love you, Jack."

He melted her at words. "I love you, too."

"No matter what happens…" She caressed his soft cheek. "We will always weather the storm."

Jack pulled her close, and after kissing her softly, he rested his forehead to hers. "Always."

EPILOGUE

RYDING HOOD

Red sucked in a breath and tugged on her dress. She hated corsets and would have been much happier wearing her leather boots and pants with a loose shirt. But it was Aria's coronation day, and the whole kingdom had turned up in their finest clothes.

The grounds had been decorated with boughs of red and white flowers. The castle had been restored, the gardens filled with lush green trees and blooms of every color. The buzz in the air was contagious. Red shouldered her way through the crowds and made for the main hall.

A guard stopped her. "Name?"

"Ryding Hood," she muttered, not bothering to add that she was mostly known as *Red*, thanks to the dumb nickname that Will Scarlet had recently given her. The guard stepped aside and she walked in, looking up at the high ceiling in awe. Ice fractals hung like chandeliers, and the stone floor was covered in snow. Jack stood tall at the front of the hall, beside the high priest.

If Red hadn't known any better, she would have thought she had stepped into a wedding. Rows of wooden benches sat on either side of the hall, leaving an aisle in the middle. Red took a seat near the front and listened to the string quartet playing a classic song.

Excited whispers flew around the hall, and Red watched Jack, who stared ahead, unmoving. He looked different. His once dark hair was white as snow, and there was something about his countenance that threw Red off. What had happened to him? He didn't look human anymore. Many rumors spread through the kingdom about Aria. One of them was that she had turned Jack into a magic snowman. She laughed to herself at that one.

But he *had* changed. Despite his serious stance, his eyes brightened and he broke into a broad grin. The song ended and a happier one picked up. Everyone rose to their feet and Red followed suit. Sighs and gasps filled the air. Red stood on her tiptoes to see over the heads, but she could only make out blonde hair.

Then she leaned to the side just as Aria passed her. Red gasped along with the other guests. She was *beautiful* with her light blue gown trailing behind her.

Aria stood at the front and kneeled down as Jack stepped aside. The high priest placed a crown on her head then handed her a golden sceptre, which she held in her right hand. When she rose, she turned around and looked out. To Red's surprise, her face was solemn and serious. There was not a hint of a smile on her red lips.

"All hail Queen Aria. May her days be long and that she reigns peacefully over the kingdom."

The guests repeated the priest's words then broke out into applause. Music played and a frosting of snow fell from the ceiling. Red held out her hand and caught the snowflakes, staring in wonderment.

Moments later, at the castle courtyard, huge banquet tables were laid out with all manner of food and drink. The guests filed into the courtyard and broke into excited chatter. Red took the opportunity to make her way out and catch up to Aria, who had already left with Jack.

"Aria, wait."

Red joined Aria on the staircase. She turned and smiled but it didn't reach her eyes. "Ry." They embraced for a moment, then she squeezed her arm as they broke apart. "What are you doing here? I thought you'd be with Robin."

"They're ready for you, my queen," one of the guards announced from the top of the staircase, and Aria turned away without so much as a goodbye. Something was wrong.

Red followed her up the staircase and to the balcony. Snow, George, and Jack were standing, waiting for her.

Red made her way to Snow as Aria stepped forward, and the sound of cheers and whistles exploded into the air. *Aria is a natural at this*, Red thought as she watched her waving her hand so delicately. She stood poised and rested a hand on the edge of the balcony while Jack looked on.

"My dear people of the Chanted Kingdom. You have suffered greatly under the reign of The Evil Queen. But now, it is time for you to finally get what you deserve."

More cheers. Aria edged next to George and put a hand on his shoulder. She leaned in and whispered something, and he responded with a puzzled look. Red wondered if it was an apology for calling his mother evil.

But then, without warning, Aria grasped his back and knocked him over the edge of the balcony. Snow gasped, grabbing Red's arm. The crowd fell into a horrified silence as the sound of George's screams were halted by a splash. Red leaned over the edge and watched in horror as the lake swallowed him up.

Jack glanced at Aria in shock, but the new queen appeared unfazed. She threw out her hands and an icy blast hit the lake, freezing it whole. Snow fell to her knees and screamed like a banshee. Aria turned away, as if unable to look. But then she sucked in a breath and straightened her posture.

"People of the Chanted Kingdom." Aria's voice boomed with authority. "The days of The Evil Queen may be over. But now, it is time for the rule of The Snow Queen."

—Before you throw this book out the window, you should know that Aria's story isn't over. Her happy ending will come, but she's got some work to do first… keeping reading the thrilling series by picking up Red Arrows now!—

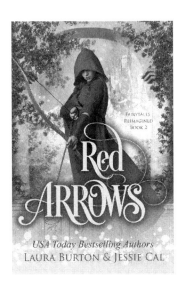

Want to share fan theories and join the Fairytales Reimagined community? Come and join us on Facebook for funny memes, games, giveaways and be the first to see cover reveals. @fairytalesreimagined

Printed in Great Britain
by Amazon